DEATH ON THE PLAINS

Wolf Who Hunts Smiling brought the buttstock up hard against the side of Matthew's head. He saw a quick burst of bright orange, then slid down out of the saddle like a heavy bag of grain.

Helpless, Matthew watched as the Cheyenne crowded around his horse and divided up everything he owned, the oldest Indian doing the distributing. After a brief speech, the brave handed the Colt to Wolf Who Hunts Smiling.

Without a word, Wolf Who Hunts Smiling calmly lifted the rifle and shot the bay in the head. The animal just missed crushing Matthew as it crumpled to the ground, blood blossoming out of its skull. When Matthew cried out, Wolf Who Hunts Smiling dismounted and pressed a razor-sharp knife against his neck.

"It has been decided. I may kill the spy to avenge my father!"

CHEYENNE #1:

ARROW KEEPER
JUDD COLE

LEISURE BOOKS   NEW YORK CITY

A LEISURE BOOK®

September 1992

Published by

Dorchester Publishing Co., Inc.
276 Fifth Avenue
New York, NY 10001

Prologue

In 1840, during the Moon When the Ponies Shed, Running Antelope of the Northern Cheyenne rode out alone into the Black Hills. There, in the sacred center of the world, the troubled Cheyenne chief unburdened his heart to the Great Spirit. For three days he danced and stared into the sun. Finally falling into a deep trance, he experienced the vision he was seeking. When he woke again, he returned to his people and called a council of all the headmen.

East of the river called Great Waters, he told them, the five nations of the Iroquois—once the mightiest of the eastern tribes—had been whipped into submission on the reservations. Soon after, the white leader Sharp Knife, who was known to his people as Andrew Jackson, spoke the lie that all land west of the Great Waters would belong to the Indians forever. But the white man's gold fever proved once again they had not spoken the straight word. The Cheyenne homeland was now swarming with Bluecoats and greedy whites. They had even begun to build a fort in the heart of the best hunting ground.

Running Antelope knew that fighting white men was like trying to stamp out a prairie fire in a windstorm. First he must try the road of peace. So when the grass was well up that year, he and 30 warriors left their stronghold on the cold-water fork of the Powder River. Running Antelope had already sent word-bringers ahead to inform their kinsmen, the Southern Cheyennes living below the Platte River, that they were arriving for a council. Running Antelope's wife, Lotus Petal, and their infant son accompanied him in order to visit her clan.

Running Antelope was a peace chief, not a war leader. Nonetheless, ignoring the white truce flag he and the warriors carried, a company of Blue-coat pony soldiers ambushed his band in a pincers movement near the North Platte.

At the first shots, Running Antelope folded his arms to show he was at peace. But the fierce pony soldiers were crazy and wild, like dogs in the Hot Moon. Cutting loose the travois to which his son was lashed, Running Antelope took the child up with him. Then he led his warriors and Lotus Petal on a desperate flight from their white attackers.

It was the Cheyenne way to flee until their pur-suers' horses faltered, then to turn and attack. But a hard winter had left their ponies weak. The braves were armed only with bows, lances, clubs, and a few single-shot muzzle-loaders. They were no match for the Bluecoats' thundering wagon guns and percussion-cap carbines.

Still, the warriors fought bravely, singing the song of battle and shouting the shrill Cheyenne war cry, *"Hiya hi-i-i-ya!"* As their horses were cut down by double charges of canister shot, they used them for breastworks and fought on. But the Cheyennes were not painted for war or wearing their crow-feather medicine bonnets, which they believed made the white man's bullets go wide. When the bloody massacre finally ended, Running Antelope, Lotus Petal, and all 30 braves lay dead or dying.

The sole survivor was the squalling infant, still clutched in the fallen chief's arms. Pawnee scouts were about to kill the child when the lieutenant in command interfered. He had the baby brought back to the riverbend settlement of Bighorn Falls near Fort Bates.

There the former fort sutler John Hanchon had opened his own mercantile store. His barren young wife Sarah instantly fell in love with the tiny orphan. Defying all warning that she would regret her decision, she insisted on raising the child as her own.

The Hanchons named him Matthew. He grew into a tall, broad-shouldered youth with the pronounced cheekbones and even, pleasing features that had earned the Cheyenne the name of the Beautiful People among their red brothers. As soon as he was old enough to be useful, Matthew began working for his father, stocking shelves and delivering orders to the fort and the few settlers in the region.

Occasionally the boy encountered hostile glances from whites in the community—particularly from frontier hard cases passing through with Indian scalps dangling from their sashes. But his parents were good to him, and he felt accepted in his limited world.

Then came his sixteenth year and a forbidden love that would leave him a homeless outcast, caught between the white man's hatred and the red man's mistrust....

Chapter 1

"God-in-whirlwinds!" said Corey Robinson when his friend Matthew Hanchon emerged through the leather-hinged front door of Hanchon's Mercantile Store. "Why, you're ready for church!"

Matthew grinned sheepishly and avoided Corey's teasing stare. He wore clean homespun trousers and a new broadcloth shirt that still felt stiff against his skin. His thick black hair had been carefully slicked back with axle grease. He was lean and straight and tall for a sixteen year old, with a strong, hawk nose and keen black eyes.

Corey's face eased into a gap-toothed smile. The pale, freckle-faced redhead was a year younger than Matthew. "Now I see which way the wind sets! You're takin' a delivery out to Hiram Steele."

"That's old news. Pa always sends me there the first of every month."

"That's so. But you never slick down your hair

when you're takin' blankets out to the fort. Course, there ain't no pretty girls to kiss at the fort, neither."

Corey dogged his friend's heels as Matthew crossed to a buckboard he had left out in the deep-rutted road just beyond the tie-rail. Behind them stood Hanchon's Mercantile, a raw plank building with a green canvas canopy. The rains had been heavy for the past several days, and duckboards had been laid out in front of the boardwalk.

Matthew checked the dry goods stacked neatly in the bed of the wagon—bolts of linsey cloth, coils of rope, a keg of nails, a drum of kerosene—against the invoice in his pocket, making sure he had loaded everything. Both boys had to squint in the bright Wyoming sunshine.

"You remember flowers for Kristen?" Corey said, grinning. "Or do you just pick 'em along the way?"

"You're standing on your grave, Sprout," Matthew warned him. He was imitating their friend Old Knobby, who worked at the feed stable. Both boys whooped with laughter and began scuffling until Sarah Hanchon's voice rang out from the doorway and pulled them up short.

"Sakes and saints, boys! Carrying on like common riffraff right out in broad daylight! You, Matthew! It's already past noon, son. Come to the house and get the silk Mr. Steele's daughter ordered special. Then you better hitch the team and get a move on. I want you back home before nightfall, hear?"

"Yes'm," Matthew said, ashamed to be scolded in front of his best friend.

"I'd best make tracks, anyway," Corey said. "Pa's preaching out at the mining camp on Sweetwater Creek. He needs me to pass the hat."

"Watch your back trail," Matthew said by way of farewell, again imitating Old Knobby.

"And you keep your nose to the wind, Hoss!"

After Corey left, Matthew stepped out of the midday glare into the dark, cluttered exterior of the store. Three walls were lined with shelves that held candles, playing cards, fishhooks, sulphur matches, needles, buttons, mirrors, jackknives, and other such merchandise. On the wall behind the broad-deal-counter hung several rifles: the new .54 caliber repeaters, breechloaders, Sam Colt's long arms with their revolving cylinders, lever-action Henry rifles.

A thickset man behind the counter was making entries in a ledger. His skin had turned pallid from working indoors since Matthew had taken over the deliveries.

"You mind your manners around Hiram Steele," John Hanchon reminded the boy without bothering to look up. "He's our best customer besides the fort."

"I know, Pa, but I hardly never see him."

"Matthew!" Sarah Hanchon's clarion voice called from within. "My lands, where are you?"

Their living quarters were connected to the store by a short dogtrot with a slab door at the house end. Matthew lifted the latch string and entered a tidy room dominated by a fieldstone fireplace. The plank floor was covered with a rose-patterned carpet. A gaudy 1856 calendar over the fireplace advertised O. F. Winchester's armaments factory.

"There you are," said Sarah, handing him a bolt of smooth blue silk. "Now you be careful with this, hear? Give it to the girl yourself, not to one of the hands. They'll get it filthy."

Matthew had to make an effort not to smile at her words. He planned to deliver it in person, all right. For a moment he felt the smooth silk, thinking of Kristen's skin and the pure bottomless blue of her eyes.

Sarah saw something in the boy's manner that made her pretty, careworn face crease in a frown. She felt a familiar gnawing of suspicion and worry.

"Matthew? You aren't being foolish about Kristen Steele, are you. Sometimes young men get silly notions about courting the wrong girls."

Matthew felt warm blood creep up the back of his neck. He loved his mother, but sometimes she said things he couldn't understand. It was as if she spoke in riddles.

"What's so foolish about me courting Kristen Steele? She don't laugh."

His words seemed to answer some unspoken question in Sarah's eyes. Still angry—and embarrassed to be talking to his mother about such private matters—Matthew said good-bye and hurried outside before she could reply.

He left the silk on the seat of the buckboard and crossed the street to a sprawling frame building with oiled paper for windows. This building was the Bighorn Falls Feed Stable, where John Hanchon boarded his two big blood bays. Matthew found Knobby in one of the empty stalls, swatting at flies with a quirt. A former mountain man, the hostler still dressed in buckskin shirt and trousers and a slouch beaver hat.

"Well, cuss my coup if it ain't young Matthew! Rest your hinder a spell, lad!"

"Can't today. Got a delivery."

12

Matthew led the gentle bloods out of their stalls. He paused to scratch the withers of a handsome pony that was contentedly chewing on a nose bag full of oats.

"Good little Injun pony," said Old Knobby, digging at a tick in his grizzled beard. "Broke by a Sioux. That-air hoss'll gallop from hell to breakfast 'n back, or I'll be et fir a tater!"

As he did at least a dozen times a day, Old Knobby proudly lifted his slouch hat to expose the hideless bone at the top of his skull. "A Cheyenne warrior damn near raised my hair and never onc't clumb off his hoss! But I reckon I let daylight into that Injun's soul!"

Knobby chuckled as he clapped his hat back on. "I'll say this much for your people, tadpole. A good brave fights meaner 'n a she-grizz with cubs."

Matthew always felt confused and uncomfortable when Knobby started that talking as if he didn't live here in town with civilized people. But, as usual, he let Knobby's remarks pass without comment.

"Keep your powder dry, pup!" Knobby called behind him as the boy led the team outside.

Matthew crossed the street and harnessed the team to the traces of the buckboard. By the time his shadow began to lengthen in the warm June sun, Matthew had left the town well behind him and was crossing the flat tableland near the Tongue River valley.

To the west, the Bighorn Mountains nosed their spires into the soft blue belly of the sky. Sunlight glinted off flakes of mica high up in the rimrock. Closer at hand, he could see the lush green gamagrass meadows that strengthened Hiram Steele's mustangs into cavalry remounts. Seeing the vast

Wyoming Territory spread out all around him like a grand painting made him quit fretting about Knobby's remark. Instead, Kristen Steele's image filled his mind's eye.

He felt butterflies stirring in his belly as he reminded himself this trip was even more special than the other visits since he and Kristen had first seen each other and fallen in love. This time he planned to ask her to marry him—not right away, of course, but in two or three years when his father's military contracts increased and he made Matthew a full partner in the store. Matthew had been raised to be practical, he knew that a man had to put by against the future if he wanted a wife and family.

Familiar with the route to the Steele's spread the team veered right when the wagon road forked near Fort Bates. And as a matter of routine, Matthew always stopped by to visit with the fort's sutler and to see if he needed anything from town. Today, he would not linger in his duties.

The fort's pine-log gun turrets soon rose into view on the horizon. A bored sentry at the main gate recognized the youth and waved him through without bothering to stop him. Matthew had just cleared the main gate when a sudden thundering of hooves erupted on his right. He reined in his team and glanced toward the parade ground in front of the enlisted barracks.

Fear instantly iced his blood and froze him motionless. For several mounted Pawnee scouts were bearing right down on him, their faces contorted as they shrieked hideously. They wore a ragtag assortment of blue Army uniforms and beaded buckskins. Their heads were shaved front and back, leaving only a knot at the crown. Those were so stiff with grease and grime, they stood straight up.

Usually the Pawnee mercenaries would stop to stare at Matthew with a hatred and cold contempt that made him avert his eyes. But that day they ignored the astonished boy. They divided and swept around the buckboard like a raging river, racing out the gate.

Slowly Matthew's heart climbed down out of his throat. Then, dumb with surprise, he realized that many of the soldiers were laughing. One of them pointed toward a fat man in tattered civilian clothes. He was wandering in aimless circles around the fort flagpole, tearing at his hair, and shouting oaths.

"It was that half-wit mule skinner what set 'em off!" a sergeant explained to his squad of gaping recruits. "We found the poor devil wandering like that out on the plains after redskins robbed and burned his freight wagon. Stow this, lads: a Pawnee figgers that a crazy-by-thunder white man is the worst bad medicine on God's green earth!"

Hoping to avoid the returning Pawnees, Matthew hurried across to the sutler's store and finished his business. An hour's ride due west of the fort brought him to the bluff overlooking Hiram Steele's bottom spread near the river. Several large pole corrals ringed the house, men working green mustangs in each. Between the notched-log house and the plank outbuildings was a long stone watering trough.

But Matthew ignored all of it. He glanced instead toward a lone stand of scrub pine that rose beyond the house where the road disappeared behind a series of grassy hummocks. His heart suddenly pounding in his ears, he urged the horses to a trot. His good mood soured, however, when he pulled into the yard and recognized the hands who were digging postholes for a new corral.

"Know what I hear, boys?" one of the hands called out, making sure Matthew could hear him. "I hear Injun bucks rut on their own mothers!"

The speaker, Boone Wilson, was long jawed and rangy, with several days' beard stubble turning his cheeks a scratchy blue black. He stared at Matthew, his eyes like pale ice. "That true, red boy? You poke your own mama?"

Matthew ignored him and started carrying the supplies into a storage lean-to off the kitchen of the main house.

"Hell, I reckon he ain't no Injun," Wilson said as Matthew swung back onto the seat. "He's what you call a red Arab of the plains!"

Derisive laughter exploding behind him, Matthew swung out onto the wagon road again. He felt Wilson's suspicious eyes on his back as he headed toward the stand of scrub pine. Some instinct warned him to look back, but he didn't. So he missed seeing Wilson head quickly up toward the house.

Matthew reined in beside a small pond and slipped the team's bits so they could drink. He found Kristen leaning against her favorite tree, her eyelids swollen and red from crying.

"What is it?" Matthew said, alarm tightening his voice.

Kristen stepped up into his arms when he opened them. She wore a pretty pink gingham dress, and her hair tumbled in a golden cascade over her shoulders. She couldn't answer him right away. For a long moment they stood silent, filled with each other. There was only the song of the lark and the whistle of the willow thrush, the distant bawling of calves. Finally Kristen could speak.

"Oh, Matthew, it's father! He's terribly angry at me. I'm frightened."

"What's this all about?"

Kristen sniffled, drawing comfort from the firm strength of Matthew's embrace. "Last week, out of the blue, he brought home a young officer from the fort, Lt. Carlson. The officer asked me to a dance at the fort, and father wants me to go."

Sudden anger and jealousy pinched Matthew's throat almost closed. "You going?"

Kristen's eyes flashed indignantly. "Of course not! I said no. But Matthew, father is more upset than I've ever seen him. I think he suspects I'm meeting someone."

"That settles it," said Matthew. "We'll tell him today."

Her eyes widened. "Tell him about us?"

"Sure. Tell him about us—and we'll tell him that today I asked you to marry me," he added on an impulse.

"You won't be telling me any such thing," rumbled a gravelly voice behind them, and Kristen cried out in fright. Matthew whirled around to confront Boone Wilson and the speaker, Hiram Steele.

"I told you, Mr. Steele," Wilson said. "I told you she was meetin' up with this Injun whelp!"

"I ain't no Injun," Matthew said hotly.

"Oh, this red varmint is all grit and a yard wide, he is," Wilson said scornfully.

Steele's hard, flint-gray eyes bored into Matthew's defiant black ones. "You better stick to your own kind."

17

Before Matthew could reply, Steele nodded to his underling. "Let's have us a huggin' match, red boy," Wilson said, stepping forward quickly.

Wilson's first punch—a vicious uppercut—slammed Matthew's head back and knocked him against the pine tree. Wilson waded in quickly, following through with several powerful punches to Matthew's face and stomach. Matthew slumped against the tree as if he'd been poleaxed. Kristen screamed when Wilson slipped a sharp Bowie knife out of the sheath on his belt. He squatted and held it right under Matthew's bloody, swelling nose.

"Next time we hug, you red devil, I'll cut you open from asshole to appetite!"

Kristen lunged toward the knife, but Steele caught her in one hand. "Put that blade away, Wilson." Holding his daughter back with one hand, he shook his other at Matthew as he said, "You've had your fair warning. I mean it, boy. Your kind is not welcome here. God have mercy on your heathen soul if I find you with my girl again."

Matthew ignored him, his eyes finding Kristen. Moving his swelling lips with difficulty, he said, "They don't matter. Do you want me to stop coming?"

Kristen's face was a study in misery. Her gaze flicked from her father's stone-eyed authority to the wicked blade Wilson was sheathing. If she said no, she realized, she was as good as killing Matthew.

"Yes," she lied.

At that moment, Matthew would have gladly welcomed Wilson's knife instead of that single word.

Chapter 2

"Damn redskins got enough guts to fill a smoke-house," said Enis McGillycuddy. "I'll be dogged and gone iffen they didn't sneak right up on our camp last night and make off with half our horses and supplies!"

Matthew was unpacking a crate of new leather harnesses and hanging them on pegs behind the broad deal counter. He watched the black-bearded miner switch his quid of chewing tobacco from his left cheek to his right. The miner's heavy, hob-nailed boots had left thick divots of dried red river clay on the bare planks of the floor. He held a scattergun loosely in his left hand, both barrels pointing down. His right fist pounded the counter as he emphasized his words to John Hanchon.

"We need more help from the fort! The Injun is a natural-born killer and thief with no respect for property rights. All this talk about learnin' 'em to farm and raise cattle is pure bosh. I wish them fancy-fine greenhorns back east could see what Injun braves does to captured white women."

John was too busy stacking supplies on the counter to reply. McGillycuddy shifted his cold, flat eyes sideways and dwelt on Matthew's bruised face, though he still directed his words to the store-keeper.

"Well, lead's going to fly. You can put *that* down in your book. There's plenty of color left in them hills, and I aim to mine it, Injuns or no, even if it comes down to the nut-cuttin'!"

His eyes still holding the boy's, he untied a leather pouch attached to his belt by a rawhide thong and shook some gold out of it. It took Matthew a moment to understand why the miner made sure he saw the pouch: it was made from a bull's scrotum.

Normally, Matthew simply ignored such hostility. But now, only a few days after the incident at Hiram Steele's, he felt heat rising to his face. Abruptly, he threw down the harness he was untangling and headed toward the dogtrot to the house.

Your kind isn't welcome here. Steele's words still burned in his memory like embers of glowing punk, their truth made all the more undeniable by Kristen's decision to reject him. Now, all the past slights and insults in his life took on a new and clearer meaning.

Stick to your own kind. Suddenly, after that humiliation, Matthew had wanted to know who he was and where he had come from. All the years of deliberate silence left him with a desire as powerful as hell thirst to solve the blank mystery of his past. He was tired of feeling like an intruding coyote.

The day before, he had finally worked up the courage to ask his father. "It's no use to lick old wounds," John had replied evasively. So Matthew knew his only hope was mother.

He found her in the bright, cheery kitchen, using the bottom of an empty whiskey bottle to press biscuits out of sourdough mash. She looked pretty and efficient in a calico skirt and soft yellow shirt-waist. Her copper hair was pulled into a tight bun on her nape.

"I thought you'd be getting hungry 'long about now," she greeted him, "judging from the food you left on your plate this morning. I'll fix you up some side meat and eggs."

Matthew shook his head. "Who was my real ma and pa?" he said bluntly.

Scarlet points appeared on his mother's pale cheeks. For nearly 16 years, she had put that question out of her mind. Now she slowly set the bottle down on the table and wiped her hands on her apron.

"Did you ask your pa that?" she said.

"Yes'm. He wouldn't tell me, though."

"Well, you just leave him alone about all that. He won't brook such questions."

"Will you tell me?"

She picked up the bottle again and vigorously resumed pressing out biscuits. "Land o' Goshen, child!" she said with false gaiety. "You will jabber on so! You'll fret me into an early grave!"

"Will you tell me?" he said. "I got a right to know."

"I knew something was troubling you," she finally said with surprising gentleness. "Especially

21

when you wouldn't tell us who you had the fight with."

She sighed, pretending great absorption in her work as she spoke. "Son, there's surely some questions it's best not to ask. The good Lord, in His infinite wisdom, saw fit to make sure your path crossed ours. You already know that an officer from Fort Bates saved you after an attack on some Cheyennes. He brought you back to town, and I fell plumb in love with you. You were such a pretty baby. And now you're a handsome young man with his whole life ahead of him. Don't dwell on the past, son."

Matthew shook his head. "Lately, seems like my whole life is behind me, and won't nobody tell me nothing. Didn't the officer at least say who my real ma and pa was?"

"We didn't want to know. All we cared about was that you were our son."

"Well then, who was that officer?"

Sarah hesitated. "He would be long gone now, Matthew, and anyway, I don't recall his name."

The tight bitterness rose in his throat before Matthew could stop it. " 'Tarnal hell! You'd think a body was askin' for the moon on a platter, close-mouthed as everybody around here is!"

"Wait, Matthew!"

But he had already stormed back into the store and past his startled father and McGillycuddy. He crossed the wide, deep-rutted street to the feed stables. He found Old Knobby in the tack room off the stables, putting calks in horseshoes.

"Heigh-up, Matthew! What's on the spit?"

The boy shrugged, suddenly tongue-tied despite his urgent need to talk.

Old Knobby slipped a bottle of whiskey from a

pair of saddlebags hanging nearby on the wall. He pulled the cork out with his few remaining teeth and took a deep swallow.

"Ahh, now that's good doin's," he said, lowering the bottle and corking it again.

"Knobby?"

"Speak up, boy, 'less you got a chicken bone caught in your throat."

"Is it true that the Injun is a natural-born thief and killer?" Matthew asked shyly.

Knobby cocked his grizzled head and gave the youth a puzzled look. " 'Pears to this hoss that you're talkin' the long way around the barn, Matthew. Spell it out plain, sprout. What's got you all consternated? Some soft-brained fool been ridin' you about your Injun blood?"

Matthew tried to speak, but the memory of his beating and humiliation and the loss of Kristen were still too fresh.

Knobby eyed the grape-colored bruise discoloring Matthew's jaw. "Blamed fool world," he muttered. "No, I don't 'spect it's true that the Injun is a natural-born killer, though they do seem to take to thievin'. It's just that the Injun's stick floats one way, the white man's another. They ain't meant to live together. The Injun figgers he belongs to the land. The white man figgers the land belongs to him. The Injun don't realize yet there ain't room in the puddle but for one big frog. And that frog is the paleface."

Matthew hung on the old man's every word. When Knobby fell silent, Matthew sat quietly considering something. Knobby peered at him closely and saw an emotion in his face that worried him.

"The Flathead tribe has got a saying, Matthew. 'Don't go lookin' for your own grave.' Whatever's eatin' at you, colt, just leave it alone. It's a bad business tryin' to mix with Injuns if you ain't been raised among 'em. Lookin' like a Cheyenne don't make you one."

"Maybe. But being raised all your life amongst the whites don't make me one of them, neither."

The bitter remark surprised Old Knobby. Although he was given to referring to the boy as an Indian, he had never heard Matthew talk about the white settlers as if he weren't one of them.

"Allasame, you just listen. Mebbe I'm old 'n all tied up with the rheumatiz. But my brain ain't gone soft yet. I can see that you got good leather in you, boy, even though you ain't got your growth yet. Some day you'll be tough as ary grizz, or I don't know gee from haw! But you can't rise up on your hind legs evertime a white man high-hats ye."

Despite his words of comfort, the old codger could see that Matthew was thinking hard and barely listening to him. Knobby sighed and shook his head.

"It's no use. Young pups is quick to say they're full dogs, I reckon. Well, daylight's burnin'. I got hosses to grain."

Knobby picked up a wide grain scoop from the nearest shelf and headed back out into the stable, and Matthew followed. When the boy reached the wide-open front doors, Knobby called out to him, and he turned around.

"Lemme give you one piece of advice. Iffen you're ever took prisoner by Injuns, and it looks like they're goin' to kill you or do something like cut off your pizzle, don't beg for mercy. Give 'em a war face and spit in their eyes to prove you ain't scairt. They'll respect you then, and you might

have a chance. They might still kill you, but least-
ways they'll do it quick.''

More a warning than a piece of advice, the old-
timer's words seemed to chase the boy out the
door. Matthew crossed the street and was abreast
his family's buckboard when something caught
the corner of his eye. He glanced sideways toward
the seat.

The bolt of blue silk looked like a luxurious cushion. He had forgotten Kristen's material. Seeing
it, Matthew felt the old warmth of love and hope
fill him for a moment. Was there still some way
to make things as they once were?

He reached out to feel the silk. But in that same
moment, he pictured Kristen's eyes after Boone
Wilson had whipped him. And it seemed clear to
him that it was shame he had read in those eyes,
not agony or love.

*The Injun's stick floats one way, the white man's
another. They ain't meant to live together.*

Lost in thought, Matthew paid little notice when
a handsome black stallion trotted up to the tie-
rail beside him. The rider swung down, the sharp-
tipped rowels of his spurs jangling, and looped his
reins. A minute later Matthew became uncom-
fortably aware that someone was standing close
to him, waiting.

He turned his head for a good look. The soldier
who stood staring back at him was no more than
20, though his sneer of cold command belied his
youth. He wore a blue uniform with yellow trim,
a saber, and a silver-gripped Colt revolver in a
stiff pistol belt. Instead of the dark blue forage cap
of an enlisted man, he wore a black-brimmed officer's hat turned up on one side. When Matthew

tried to move around him, the officer stepped with him, trapping him.

"The name is Carlson," he said. "Lt. Seth Carlson, Seventh Cavalry. I had a visit last night from a concerned citizen named Boone Wilson. He informed me of some matters I definitely did not want to hear."

Again Matthew tried to edge around the officer. And again Carlson blocked him.

"I'm going to add my warning to Hiram Steele's," the lieutenant said. "You steer good and clear of Kristen. She's spoken for. But even if she wasn't, she's a white woman. So you just steer good and clear, hear?"

Until that moment, Matthew had had no plans to see Kristen again. His pride would not let him beg after she had told him she did not want to see him. But the arrogant, blue-eyed fool angered him. Lately he had his belly full of threats.

"Kristen and I will do what we damn well aim to do," said Matthew. "And the fact is we aim to get married."

When he heard Matthew's response, Carlson flushed so deep with rage that his earlobes turned pink. This time when he tried to stop Matthew from stepping around him, Matthew shoved him back hard. Enraged, Carlson swung a fast right hook at him. But he was still off balance from Matthew's push, and his punch was only a glancing blow.

Suddenly, Matthew's anger rose up out of him with the force of an explosion. He set his legs for good balance and punched hard, driving a fast right fist into Carlson's stomach. He followed with a left that smashed the officer's lips. Another hard right to the jaw left Carlson sprawling among the wagon ruts in the road. Then he slowly shook his head like a confused bull, clearing his vision.

Swaying slightly, the soldier stood up. His pistol was halfway out of its holster when both he and Matthew heard the loud click of a hammer being cocked. They stared across the street. Knobby stood in the doorway of the feed stable, a long Kentucky flintlock aimed at the officer.

"Do it, shavetail," said Knobby, "and you'll be shovelin' coal in hell!"

After a long moment, Carlson's hand came away empty from his pistol belt. But as he dusted himself off, he spoke in a low voice that only Matthew could hear.

"In case you haven't heard, there's a new mercantile going up over in Red Shale. I know the owner, and so does my commanding officer. There's nothing carved in stone that guarantees John Hanchon's contract with Fort Bates. Way I and some others see it, why should the army take its business to those who feed and clothe its enemies?"

The clear threat in this remark left Matthew numb. Without a word, he watched the officer mount his horse and ride out of town at a canter. His face grim with worry, Matthew turned back to the buckboard and reached for the silk.

Abruptly, he dropped his hand and left the cloth where it was. After all, he told himself bitterly, it would only end up as a fancy dress Kristen would wear to please her young officer.

After that day, Matthew realized, he would be making no more deliveries for his father. The set-to with Carlson was the last straw. It was bad enough to be told he didn't belong. But when the man and woman who had raised him began to be

27

threatened with ruin because of him, he had no choice.

The decision had just been made for him—Matthew knew what he had to do.

Getting through the rest of the day felt to Matthew like acting in a play. Matthew stocked goods, delivered supplies to the Widow Johnson's place on Sweetwater Creek, and took his supper with his parents, just as on any other day. But when his ma kissed his cheek that night at bedtime, he felt as if a knife were twisting into his guts.

Long before midnight, the town of Bighorn Falls was as silent and dark and still as a prairie graveyard. Matthew sat up wide awake in his cramped cubbyhole off the kitchen, writing in the flickering light of a tiny candle stub. He wanted to explain the confused knot of feelings inside him. But when he couldn't find the words, he gave up and settled for a short note.

Dear Father and Mother,
I love both of you very much. You always been so good to me. But theres too many others who don't feel the way you do. Others who might hurt you because of me. I am sick and tired of being treated like a animal. I am sorry I cant do a good job of telling you what it is I feel. But I have to go find out if theres some other place where I belong. Pa, I will try to send money someday for the bay and the rifle I took.
Your loving son,
Matthew

He moved silently, wincing every time a floorboard or joist creaked. Matthew spread his slicker open on the bed. Then he tiptoed into the larder and took hardtack, biscuits, beans, and jerked beef. He wrapped these in cheesecloth, then placed the bundle in the slicker, along with a few sulphur matches, some coffee, and his new calfskin boots. He bundled up the oil-treated cloth and moved out front to the store.

Matthew had an old .33 caliber breechloader he used for hunting rabbits. But he left it, selecting instead a Colt Model 1855 percussion rifle. He also took a bore brush, gun oil, caps, and powder. He filled a buckskin pouch with lead balls and piled everything on the counter. As an afterthought, he added a canteen.

A few minutes later, he was easing the double doors of the stable open, frowning when the weathered wood groaned like a man in pain. Pale moonlight slanted through the open loft window over the doors, illuminating the shadow-mottled interior in a ghostly light. One of the horses whickered, and the sound startled Matthew. But Knobby's steady snoring from up in the loft went on in an uninterrupted cadence. The strong smell of whiskey stained the manure-fragrant air.

Matthew made his way slowly to the tack room, feeling his way in the near darkness of the interior. He groped until he found an old saddle and bridle Knobby had tossed into a back corner. Matthew knew Knobby wouldn't begrudge him them—not after all the work he had done for the old hostler.

He lugged the saddle and bridle back into the stable and dropped the tack long enough to back one of the bays out of its stall. The friendly animal nosed his shoulder and Matthew patted its neck.

When he slipped the bridle on, the bay easily took the bit.

Matthew threw the saddle blanket on, then the saddle, and cinched the thongs. His heart finally starting to pound hard as the moment for departure neared, he led his horse across to the store's tie-rail and looped the reins around it.

After retrieving his poke and weapon from inside, Matthew slid the rifle into the saddle scabbard and lashed his belongings behind the cantle with rawhide whangs. Then, his reluctant legs as heavy as solid stone, he went back into the house and paused in his parents' open doorway.

Moonlight outlined both of them in a soft glow like foxfire. His mother's pretty, normally fretful face was almost fey and girlish in repose, as if years of hard work had been soothed away. And his father's seamed, honest face—the face of a good man who had always done right by Matthew and everyone he dealt with—looked younger too.

The boy was ashamed when his eyes abruptly trembled and the hot tears came. But Carlson's words lashed his memory like a relentless whip, goading him into action. *There's nothing carved in stone that guarantees John Hanchon's contract with Fort Bates.*

Matthew wiped his eyes with the back of one hand. Then he hardened himself for whatever lay ahead. He cast a final glance at the only family he had ever known and left his home for the last time. He unlooped the reins and stepped up into leather. Then, his heart saddened but determined, he pointed bridle north toward the Powder River and Cheyenne country.

Chapter 3

For nearly a week, Matthew rode from sunup to sunset, his only destination the upcountry of the Powder River. He had no firm plan. But like a buffalo following the ancient stampede trails, he stubbornly held his course.

His first two days on the move were warm and dry, and he made good time. But early on the third day, the seamless blue sky turned the color of dull pewter and for two days, thick gray sheets of rain poured down without letting up. It was impossible to find dry wood for a fire. At night, teeth chattering, Matthew wrapped himself in his blanket and slicker, then burrowed deep into fallen leaves to keep warm.

As the rains continued, the rivers and creeks of the Northeast Wyoming Territory, already swollen with spring runoff from the mountains, became treacherous to cross. Once, at the Shoshone

River, Matthew was forced to backtrack downstream to a less turbulent spot where the bay would not shy when he coaxed him close to the raging waters.

To make matters worse, he had stupidly forgotten to bring a knife for skinning small game. To supplement his hardtack and jerked beef, he picked green but edible wild plums and serviceberries.

At one point, where the western edge of the Black Hills bordered the plain, he was forced to run to high ground for hours while a huge buffalo herd stampeded by. Fascinated, he watched hundreds of wolves worrying the fringes of the herd, weeding out sick, lame, and aged buffalo.

As he traveled, Matthew saw his first grizzly. It emerged from a cave near Beaver Creek, a huge, brownish-yellow male with long, curved claws the length of a grown man's foot. It rose up to its full height on its hind legs, sniffing the wind and making deep growling sounds. Matthew was grateful he was downwind. But he also prayed that Old Knobby had been right when he told the boy a grizzly's eyes were as weak as a buffalo's.

Matthew spotted plenty of mule deers and big gray prairie wolves at lower altitudes, and elk and bighorn sheep higher up. But people were scarce, which suited him fine. He saw miners occasionally, and twice he happened upon small details of soldiers cutting logs for new forts. Once, skirting the banks of the southern Powder River, he saw a large keelboat loaded with whiskey. But he avoided everyone he saw.

Late on the fifth day of his journey, crossing a high ridge between the Powder and the Tongue, he spotted another detail of soldiers cutting pine

logs in the valley of the Powder. Sunlight glinted
off a sentry's field glasses as he studied the lone
rider. No doubt puzzled at recognizing a lone Indian dressed as a white man, the soldiers sent a
detail racing toward his position to investigate.

Matthew reminded himself these weren't soldiers from Fort Bates who knew him. That
thought made him abruptly rein his mount down
the backside of the ridge. As he rode, he suddenly
heard thwacking noises everywhere. Moments
later he recognized the hard sounds as lead balls
crashing into trees. Turning around on his mount,
he saw the soldiers firing upon him and realized
the bullets were reaching him before the sound of
gunfire!

The squad of cavalry guards charged him.
Though he had a good lead, the soldiers' horses
were strong and well rested. Matthew rode his
tired bay hard, but it was lathered quickly from
the pace. He had no choice but to hide in a river
thicket until the soldiers gave up their search. Afterwards, he slipped the bay's bit and loosened
the cinch, letting his thirsty mount drink from the
river. Since Matthew's legs and back ached from
the saddle, he decided to camp right there.

That night, burrowing deep into the leaves under a moon as round and ripe as a melon, he
thought about the meaning of the soldier's actions.
They considered him an enemy, just one more
Cheyenne buck to slaughter. Out on the open
plain, he was no longer the son of John And Sarah
Hanchon, respected citizens of Bighorn Falls.

As he lay there in the country of the Northern
Cheyennes, the foolish desperation of his plan suddenly became painfully obvious. Old Knobby was
right, he told himself: He couldn't simply ride up

to a Cheyenne camp and expect to be accepted as a member. Besides, almost a week with no human company under the big, lonesome dome of sky made him feel lonesome and small. He missed the people back home—especially Kristen. His brain tangled by such thoughts, he finally drifted off to sleep.

The next morning he risked a fire long enough to boil coffee. Then he walked down closer to the river, where he had tethered the bay in a good patch of graze. He led the horse back to his camp, saddled him, and cinched the girth under his belly. For the next few hours, he followed the Powder as it wound northeast.

Toward noon, plunging up the side of a cutbank, the bay suddenly shied. And sweat broke out on Matthew's back when he spied four armed Cheyenne sitting their ponies directly across his path.

There was a long, surprised silence on both sides. The Cheyenne stared, their faces impassive, but their eyes revealing shock at the sight of this towering young Cheyenne dressed in white man's clothing. Three of them were full-grown braves older than Matthew. The fourth was a few years younger. They wore beaded leggings, breech-clouts, and elkskin moccasins. Their weapons included streamered battle lances, bows and arrows, sturdy British trade rifles known as Indian guns and London fusils. Two of the braves wore leather bands on their wrists for protection from the slap of bowstrings. All of them rode their mustangs bareback, except for the thin cushion of red Hudson Bay blankets.

Their hair was longer than Matthew's, hanging in loose locks, but cut off close above the brows to keep their vision clear. Matthew knew, from all of Knobby's stories, that the pouches hanging from buckskin thongs on their breechclouts were their medicine bags. These held pieces of the special totem, or magic object, for each man's clan. Knobby had told of seeing beaks, claws, feathers, and precious stones in different medicine bags.

Matthew wondered why the older Cheyenne also had pieces of coarse horse tail dangling from their waists—until he realized they were scalps. Then his blood ran cold.

Finally, the oldest brave rode close enough to touch the bay's nose. He said something in a strange language that was mere gibberish to the youth.

Unsure what to do, Matthew finally offered his right hand. "How do you do?" he said. "My name is Matthew Hanchon."

The brave stared at the hand, contempt starched into every feature. Behind him, the others broke into gales of hearty laughter.

"How do you do?" one of them said awkwardly, offering his hand to another. Both braves laughed so hard they had to slide down from their horses and roll on the ground.

As his friends laughed, the brave who had ridden forward allowed his face to show his hatred for the Indian who had traded his breechclout and moccasins for trousers and boots. He wheeled his pony around and returned to his companions. After a brief conference, the youngest Cheyenne rode forward. He had a wily face and swift, furtive eyes that watched Matthew's every move.

"I am called Wolf Who Hunts Smiling," he said proudly in slow but good English. "My father was Red Feather of the Panther Clan. I belong to Yellow Bear's band."

"You speak English!" said Matthew, relieved.

"For two winters, I and my father were prisoners of the Long Knives at the soldier's house called Fort Laramie. We escaped, but my father was killed by the big-talking guns."

His words were as flat and hate-filled as his eyes. "Why have you ridden into our country?" he demanded.

Matthew swallowed the hard lump in his throat. For the first time he finally had to admit his purpose. "Because I am a Cheyenne, and I want to be with my own people."

A sneer divided Wolf Who Hunts Smiling's face. He called something back over his shoulder to the rest, and they laughed again.

"You, a *Shaiyena!*" said Wolf Who Hunts Smiling. "You who offer us your hand to shake like the Bluecoat liars who shake the red man's hand before they kill him and take his land? I say you are a double-tongued spy sent to listen and learn. Everyone knows that the Bluecoats use Indian spies to discover our camps."

"No! I swear I'm not."

"I have no ears to hear your lies, white man's dog!"

Wolf Who Hunts Smiling abruptly wheeled his pony around and approached his companions again. After a brief exchange with the other braves, he returned, his eyes glinting with triumph.

"I told them you are a spy who pretends not to know our language. The rest agree."

Without another word Wolf Who Hunts Smiling leaned forward, hugging his mustang's neck between his knees. To Matthew's surprise, he slid the new Colt out of the saddle scabbard.

When Matthew instinctively reached out to grab the weapon back, Wolf Who Hunts Smiling brought the buttstock up hard against the side of the youth's head. He saw a quick burst of bright orange, then he slid down out of the saddle like a heavy bag of grain.

Matthew never quite lost consciousness, but his limbs felt like stones he could not lift. Helpless, he watched from the ground as the Cheyenne crowded around his horse and divided up everything he owned, the oldest Indian doing the distributing. After a brief speech, the brave handed the Colt to Wolf Who Hunts Smiling.

Without a word, Wolf Who Hunts Smiling calmly lifted the rifle and shot the bay in the head. The animal just missed crushing Matthew as it crumpled to the ground, blood blossoming out of its skull. When Matthew cried out, Wolf Who Hunts Smiling dismounted and pressed a razor-sharp knife against his neck.

"It has been decided. I may kill the spy to avenge my father!"

White-hot fire creased Matthew's neck as the young Indian pressed the blade into his flesh, drawing blood. His tormentor's lupine face twisted with scorn as he watched the fear show in the youth's eyes!

As Wolf Who Hunts Smiling flexed his arm to press the blade deeper, Matthew remembered Knobby's advice. His eyes registering defiant hate instead of fear, he hawked up a wad of phlegm and spat it in his adversary's face.

Momentarily startled, Wolf Who Hunts Smiling loosened his pressure on the blade. Matthew had recovered enough strength to arch his strong back and throw the younger and smaller Cheyenne clear. But as he rose to his knees, one of the braves clubbed him with a heavy trade rifle, knocking him unconscious. With a triumphant shriek, Wolf Who Hunts Smiling leapt at the boy, his knife held high. But the oldest brave caught his arm in an iron grip.

"Brothers!" he said. "You saw the tall stranger's courage just now. Could we be wrong? His blood is *Shaiyena*. An acorn wrapped in a leaf is still an acorn, not a leaf. Will we shed the blood of our own as quickly as the Bluecoats do? I say we must take him back before the council."

"No, War Bonnet, he is a spy for the whites," Wolf Who Hunts Smiling protested. "The whites killed my father. My heart is like a stone toward them. I say we kill him!"

"Does the calf bellow to the bull? Are you a warrior whose words weigh with mine?" War Bonnet demanded. Wolf Who Hunts Smiling looked away, his face contrite but still angry.

"You know I speak only the straight word! In the Crooked Lance Clan, we have been forced to fight and kill many enemies, but we kill none who do not fire at us first. We will take the stranger back with us and let the headmen decide his fate!"

Chapter 4

Later that afternoon, the four Cheyenne returned to their tribe's summer camp at the fork where the Little Powder joined the Powder. His face stern but proud, Wolf Who Hunts Smiling led their packhorse by a lariat. The animal pulled a travois to which their prisoner, who had regained consciousness, had been lashed. Matthew's legs had been left to bounce over the rough, rocky ground, in the course of the journey, they had been badly bloodied and bruised. In addition, one of his eyes had swollen shut from the impact of the trade rifle's butt.

The entire village gathered at a huge open area surrounding the Council Lodge. The Indians stared, some more surprised than hostile, as the prisoner was lashed to a carved pole from which dangled enemy scalps.

For the rest of that day and through the night,

Matthew was deliberately ignored by the men of the tribe. Occasionally, a small, naked child would dart forward to poke at him with a stick or yank his hair. Once, an old squaw, her wrinkled face twisted with hate at the sight of Matthew's white man's clothing, spat contemptuously in his face. A few of the younger females were less hostile toward the handsome prisoner—even openly curious when no elders were about to scold them for looking. One in particular found excuses to pass by him several times on various errands.

Despite his fear and the pain from his wounds, Matthew was struck by the frail beauty of the maiden's high, finely sculpted cheekbones. She was clearly different from the other girls her age. While most of the young women in the tribe wore glittery beads, buttons or shells in their hair, her long black hair was braided only with white petals of mountain columbine. Her buckskin dress, which was decorated with elk teeth and eagle tails, had gold coins for buttons. Her bare legs were the color of wild honey.

From his position at the middle of camp, Matthew watched the entire village. The tipis, erected in circles by clans, were covered with tanned buffalo hides. Many had worn so thin they were bright with the cooking fire within. Dark plumes curled out the smoke holes.

A crude pole corral beyond the camp was filled with well-fed ponies and mules. Closer at hand, Matthew could see a group of women huddled around a huge side of fresh buffalo meat. They cut razor-thin slices and stretched them on pole racks to dry. Amazed, Matthew watched children old enough to walk still nursing at their mothers' breasts as the women went about their tasks.

By the time darkness descended, fires crackled and blazed everywhere. Cramped and uncomfortable in his sitting position, Matthew realized that, unlike Bighorn Falls, the Cheyenne village had no official bedtime. Because it was noisy and active all night long, he slept little. Children played, braves bet on pony races through the middle of camp, and old women with their hair cut short in mourning chanted all night long.

The only thing Matthew craved more than sleep was food. It wasn't until well past midnight that an old squaw approached him carrying a piece of bark with cooked meat on it. Her face stony and impassive, she held it up so he could eat.

Although the meat was tough and stringy, he chewed ravenously and ignored the queer taste. Only after he had swallowed most of it did the old squaw shift her position enough for him to see the carcass of a young dog on the spit behind her. The old squaw cursed and leapt back when Matthew suddenly retched up the meat. Her eyes were bright with contempt for the weak white man's Indian who stupidly wasted such a delicacy.

Thoroughly miserable, homesick, and frightened, Matthew finally drifted into an uneasy sleep near dawn. Far too soon, he was shaken roughly awake by another old squaw with a face as cracked and lined as the clay of a long-dry riverbed. This one brought him a strip of dried venison, which he devoured as quickly as she could shove it into his mouth.

Most of the fires had burned down to embers. Even though it was not yet midmorning, Matthew saw plenty of activity around the Council Lodge, and he knew he was the cause of it. This central structure, which consisted of a wooden frame cov-

41

ered with elk and buffalo hides, was the largest in the camp.

Matthew had not been watching the lodge long when a lone horseman rode throughout the camp, shouting something over and over like a town crier. Men emerged from tipis and filed inside the council lodge, still carefully avoiding any glances toward him. They wore their best ornamental garments for the council. They were decorated with porcupine quills, stones, feathers, leather fringes, and hair from enemy scalps.

As the adult males entered the Council Lodge, Wolf Who Hunts Smiling and two braves approached Matthew.

"We will both attend the council," Wolf Who Hunts Smiling said coldly. "It is customary that only warriors are permitted. But you must be there to hear the Council judgment, and I must be there to be your tongue."

When Wolf Who Hunts Smiling finished speaking, one of the braves thrust his stone lance point into Matthew's neck while the other untied his hands. But their precautions were wasted, for Matthew was so cramped from his position that one of the braves was forced to help him to his feet.

The Council Lodge was packed. Each clan had sent its Headmen, and they sat in a circle that took up half of the structure. In their midst reigned Chief Yellow Bear in a red blanket, his silver hair flowing over his shoulders. The other half of the lodge was filled with adult braves who were permitted to speak, but not to vote on Matthew's fate.

All eyes stared at Matthew as he was led to the center of the lodge and told to sit. Next to him, Wolf Who Hunts Smiling explained all that took

place. Chief Yellow Bear stuffed a clay pipe with
kinnikinnick. Before he smoked, the chief pointed
the pipe to all the directions of the wind and to
the sun, the moon, and the sky. When he had in-
haled the mixture of tobacco and red willow bark,
he passed the pipe on.

Soon the sweet, fragrant smell of burning willow bark filled the lodge. When the councillors had
finished smoking, an old man called Medicine Bottle chanted a prayer. Normally the official tribal
medicine man Arrow Keeper would perform that
duty. But he had departed seven sleeps earlier for
a fasting ceremony at distant Medicine Lake.

"Brothers!" Yellow Bear said when the prayer
was finished. "We are called here today to decide
the fate of this stranger. He rides into our country
calling himself a Cheyenne, but speaks the language of the Long Knives. Let us first hear his story
and decide if we can place his words near our
hearts."

"He is a white man in his manner and bearing.
No white man has ever talked one way to the In-
dian," protested a young warrior named Black
Elk. "They are all liars. Kill him now!"

A murmur of approval from the other young
warriors greeted the remarks. When Black Elk's
murderous black eyes met Matthew's, the prisoner
shuddered. One of the warrior's ears had been partially torn off and sewn back onto his skull with
buckskin thread. The wound made Black Elk appear as fierce as his words.

"Black Elk speaks as if he has drunk the white
man's devil water," Yellow Bear said. "Let the
prisoner talk first!"

Halting often so that Wolf Who Hunts Smiling
could translate, Matthew did his best to explain

his situation. But with all those hostile faces turned toward him, it was impossible to describe how he felt about Kristen—or how he felt as if a knife was twisting in his guts when white men treated him like an animal.

"His words do not ring with truth!" Black Elk insisted upon hearing Matthew's story. "The white men are foxes who do not want peace. They send their spies among us to learn our plans. I say we kill him now!"

Again the younger warriors greeted his talk with shouts and raised fists. Yellow Bear folded his arms until they grew quiet. Turning to Medicine Bottle, he asked, "What is it you advise?"

Old Medicine Bottle was silent a long time before he spoke. At last, he said, "Brothers! I counsel as Arrow Keeper himself would, and I counsel for mercy. This stranger who arrives among us has *Shaiyena* blood coursing through his veins. True, he has been contaminated by living among our enemies, but even among the whites are some good, honorable men. Did I not see with my own eyes how a young Bluecoat officer was killed by his eagle chief for refusing to fire on our women and children? It is useless to fight the white men. Their numbers are like the locusts."

"No!" Black Elk shouted. "We must drive the white men from the mountains of the bighorn sheep. We must save the valley of our river. We have no other hunting grounds left to us. I speak for my young cousin Wolf Who Hunts Smiling and many others present who saw our fathers and mothers slaughtered. We hate the whites even more than we hate the Pawnee and the Crows and the Ute. We must raise our battle-axes against them until death. This one stinks like the whites who sent him to spy!"

When the lodge erupted in an uproar, Yellow Bear folded his arms and waited for silence. When it didn't come, he shook his fist and shouted above the din.

"Brothers! I have rinsed my mouth in cold, fresh water, and now I speak only true things. How many times have I cut short my hair for our dead? Have I not heard my brave wife Little Raven sing the Death Song because of a Bluecoat bullet?

"Hear me well, brothers! Yellow Bear has eaten his fill of this ugly poison called killing. He will never shed Cheyenne blood with his own hand. But let the headmen speak with their stones, for I have spoken and can say no more."

Matthew watched, his mouth a straight, determined slit, as Medicine Bottle passed a fur pouch among the 20 voting headmen. The pouch contained 40 small stones. Each councillor reached in and removed the stone of his choice—a white moonstone or a black agate—keeping it hidden in his hand.

When he had made the rounds, Medicine Bottle handed the half-empty pouch to Chief Yellow Bear. Yellow Bear grabbed it by the bottom and emptied it on the buffalo robe at his feet.

Twenty stones spilled out—a few white, but most of them black agates.

For the first time Yellow Bear looked directly at the prisoner. Deep lines like cracked leather ran from the corner of the old chief's eyes, which seemed saddened by some grief that could not be spoken.

"My young men are thirsty for blood. Like their chief, my old men counsel mercy. But the headmen wisely understand. If we elders always turn stone ears to our young warriors, they will rebel and follow their own leaders. The headmen know that sometimes the old trees must bend so the new trees can grow straight. Now the tribe has spoken with one voice."

The sadness suddenly left Yellow Bear's eyes, and they turned hard as flint as ancient duty took over. He announced something else, and when Wolf Who Hunts Smiling turned to Matthew to translate, the young Cheyenne's face glowed with triumph.

"Yellow Bear says the stones have spoken. You are a spy for the whites, and you must die!"

Chapter 5

The Pawnee scout named Fleet Foot stepped quietly ashore and lugged his log dugout up onto the bank. He stashed it under a nearby deadfall of tangled branches. As he moved cautiously away from the Powder, a flock of small sandpipers rose in a sudden flurry. Fleet Foot stopped dead still, fully aware that a sentry from Yellow Bear's camp might easily notice the sign. But he relaxed again when the familiar Cheyenne wolf howl of alarm failed to sound.

The scout wore his hair in the distinctive fashion of his tribe—shaved everywhere except for a stiff top-knot. He was well armed, for he did not come on a mission of friendship. If he were spotted, he would have to fight for his life. Besides a bow strung with buffalo sinew and arrows in a stiff leather quiver he carried an old .33 caliber Hawken rifle, its badly cracked stock wrapped tight in buckskin to strengthen it. In addition, he had lashed a spiked tomahawk to his legging sash.

For many sleeps, he had traveled north by himself, always staying ahead of the main Pawnee band. Living on dried venison and bitterroot, he avoided Cheyenne, Sioux, and Arapahoe hunters and messengers even as he gained valuable information on their camps.

Confident he was still undetected by his enemies, Fleet Foot resumed his trek away from the river. His quilled moccasins were silent on the forest floor. The experienced scout moved slowly, knowing it was movement, not shape, that would catch an enemy's eye. Flies and mosquitoes bit him mercilessly, and he wished he could build a smudge fire to smoke them off.

On a well-traveled game trail, he crouched to read the prints. Fleet Foot knew how to identify any Indian tribe by its moccasins. These prints told him that only Cheyenne had passed by that way recently. He also read the tracks of muskrats, weasels, and wolves and hungry cougars down from the mountains to feast on fat mule deer or elk. A set of fresh pony prints—no doubt made earlier that morning by the departing Cheyenne hunters—led away from the camp, but did not return. So the hunters were still out for the day. Fleet Foot knew he must be cautious, to prevent his path from crossing theirs.

He was upwind of the camp, and that worried him. Cheyenne dogs were trained to hate the distinctive smell of the Pawnee. To avoid detection, Fleet Foot had earlier saturated his moccasins, clothing, and skin in the smoke of cedar and sage.

As he parted the leaves of a thicket and peered out at the camp circles in the grassy clearing, a wicked smile touched his lips. He realized why it had been so easy to sneak up on the camp unchallenged. Everyone—except one bored old squaw who hunkered in front of her tipi, finishing a hide on pumice stone—was distracted by the entertaining spectacle in the middle of camp.

A wagon wheel and axle, perhaps the remnants of a raid on soldiers or white settlers, had been rigged into the fork of a huge cottonwood. The wheel was free to spin a few feet above a smoldering bed of embers. Lashed to the wheel was a broad-shouldered Cheyenne youth dressed in the torn, bloodied clothing of a white man.

As Fleet Foot watched, a brave spun the wheel until the prisoner's bare feet were only inches above the glowing embers. His face crumpled in pain, the prisoner screamed and strained against the buffalo-hair ropes, uselessly trying to raise his feet.

Fleet Foot watched calmly. Unaffected by the scene before him, he picked lice out of the grease on his top-knot and cracked them between his teeth. Studying the area surrounding the camp carefully, the Pawnee made an inner map of all the best positions from which his tribe could launch fire arrows at the lodges and tipis. He was especially careful to note the size and position of the corral, because the Cheyenne were renowned for having the best horses on the plains.

Another scream below split the stillness. Fleet Foot regretted that the main body of Pawnee was still many sleeps to the south. Now would be a perfect time for the attack. But it would come soon enough.

With nothing else at the moment to do, he settled in to witness the outcome of the prisoner's punishment.

Matthew felt the world spinning again, then the white-hot stabbing of horrible pain in his feet. Against his will he screamed.

The ground and the sky were flip-flopped once more as the wheel was turned. With his face hanging near the incredible heat, he smelled the putrid stink of his hair burning. His face began to blister as he endured pain worse than any he had ever known.

Then, mercifully, the pain eased a bit as the brave who controlled the wheel momentarily turned him away from the heat. Through eyes filled with involuntary tears, Matthew saw the entire tribe watching him. Oddly, as he gazed at the Indians he had no fear of dying. Rather, he felt sadness and anger at having failed in his plan— and at the prospect of dying as an outcast in both the white man's world and the red man's.

Matthew was too weakened by the torture to notice that the pretty maiden with white columbine in her hair was watching him again. Her lower lip was caught between her strong white teeth in distress. But Yellow Bear did notice her concern, and the old chief's heart was heavy with apprehension. For she was his daughter Honey Eater, and it was not her way to bother with the young bucks. She was aloof and reserved even around her most zealous admirer, Black Elk—a bold and proud suitor who did not take kindly to any slights. Her concern for a suspicious stranger, Yellow Bear thought, was an alarming omen. What it foretold he dared not wonder.

Although Yellow Bear had never been fond of

torture, he sadly realized it was sometimes necessary. Tribal law demanded it before a spy was killed and his scalp added to the pole near the medicine lodge.

Sharp Lance, the brave turning the wagon wheel, suddenly grabbed a spoke and gave the wheel a quarter turn. Matthew's blistered feet moved within inches of the glowing embers. He could not help screaming as the sweet stink of scorched flesh rose to his nostrils. Every muscle in his body corded tight as he strained to break his bonds.

The girl named Honey Eater sought her father's eyes and begged him to stop the torture. His seamed old face as impassive as stone, he finally parted his blanket with one hand and raised his fist high.

"Enough!" he said in a commanding tone. He removed a bone-handle knife from the sheath at his waist. "Brothers, hear me well. The warm moons are a time for communing with the Great Spirit, for beseeching His pity and seeking visions. Let us have many hunts and dances before the coming of the cold moons, and leave this bloody, unhappy day behind us!"

His slitted eyes turned to Black Elk, the fiercest of the young warriors. Black Elk had counted coup on more Bluecoats than the rest of the young warriors, and already his bonnet was full of the eagle feathers of bravery. Without a word Yellow Bear handed him the knife. Then the chief folded his arms and faced away from the prisoner. He had to support the tribe's decision and stay through the execution; but his gesture expressed his disapproval of one Cheyenne drawing the blood of another.

Judd Cole

Matthew's mind played cat and mouse with consciousness as excruciating pain washed over him in red, throbbing waves. He was still aware enough to notice when Yellow Bear unsheathed the knife, and the searing agony made him welcome the prospect of death.

He saw the old chief turn his back. After a pause War Bonnet followed Yellow Bear's example and turned his back too. A few others, including old Medicine Bottle, joined them. After that, Matthew's body sagged against the ropes and he passed out.

Black Elk gripped the bone handle of the knife, blood in his eyes as he recalled the Bluecoat saber that had nearly severed his ear. But instead of plunging the knife into the prisoner, he sought his young cousin Wolf Who Hunts Smiling out of the crowd and called him forward.

"Avenge your father," Black Elk said, handing the knife to the younger Cheyenne.

Wolf Who Hunts Smiling stared hard at the unconscious spy, nervous despite his eagerness. The execution would be his first scalp. He knew how it was done, of course, from watching the warriors. The process was simple. He had to put his foot on the enemy's neck or face. Then, after making an outline around the skull, he simply had to snap the scalp loose in a powerful, thrusting jerk.

As hundreds of eyes watched him expectantly, Wolf Who Hunts Smiling slashed the hair ropes and Matthew slumped onto the ground. His eyes gleaming with keen triumph, the young Cheyenne placed one foot on the spy's neck and knelt to take his trophy.

Chapter 6

Arrow Keeper of the Northern Cheyenne felt stiff and exhausted when he finally left sacred Medicine Lake to return to Yellow Bear's tribe. But he was also profoundly moved by the vision he had received.

Arrow Keeper, whose medicine bundle was the owl, was older even than Chief Yellow Bear. His long hair had slowly turned to gray streaked with white. His ancient but distinguished face was as weathered and wrinkled as an old apple core.

He carried no weapons, relying only on magic and the benevolent will of the Great Spirit to protect him. For his special journey to the sacred lake, he wore a magic panther skin, which gave him such strong medicine that not a single bullet could touch him. He also carried a magic bloodstone that made it difficult for his enemies to find his tracks.

He had left the lake when his uncle the moon began creeping down from its zenith in the sky. For three days, he had stood in water up to his neck, staring into the sun. On the third day the vision came.

But the cool water and his advanced age had exacted their tribute. Before he could mount and ride out, the old man found it necessary to rub boiled sassafras on his stiff limbs. When he was able to ride, he let his piebald pony set its own pace along a game trail, and he carefully avoided the Bluecoat wagon track nearby. After a two-day ride, Arrow Keeper had almost completed the journey from the isolated mountain lake to Yellow Bear's summer camp. But even as he drew near his home, he had been forced to swing wide around Bear Creek to avoid the new Soldier Town with its formidable walls of squared-off cottonwood logs.

Bluecoats were not the only intruders there in the midst of the best Cheyenne hunting grounds. Arrow Keeper had also been forced to backtrack to avoid a huge party of white hiders. To the old Cheyenne's horror, they had slaughtered hundreds of buffalo and skinned them with their strange curved knives, staking the hides out to flatten them. Arrow Keeper shook his silvered head sadly. Besides the hides and tongues, which the hiders cut out and packed in brine, the whitemen had no use for the other parts of the once mighty beasts; so the carcasses were left to rot in the sun. Wasted were the fat and delicious bone marrow that could be used for cooking, the sinews that would make strong thread. Spoons and cups could have been made from the horns, ropes and belts woven from the hair. Instead, the gifts of the Great Spirit were squandered.

Despite the fact that he thought the white men were intruders, and that nothing good could come of their arrival in the land, the old medicine man also believed that the same Great Spirit who made the Cheyenne must have made the white men. Unlike most in Yellow Bear's tribe, Arrow Keeper found many things to admire about the whites. Like the Indians, they could be brave, dangerous warriors—especially when they were fighting to protect their families.

And their own magic was powerful. Arrow Keeper had seen the smoke-belching iron horses east of the Great Waters, and he had heard rumors of the new talking wires that would soon carry words through the sky like lightning bolts. But he could never understand or trust a race that wasted good meat, ruined a horse's flanks with sharp-roweled spurs, and gave strong water to the red man because they knew it would destroy him.

However, the old Cheyenne could not think long about such things. For his mind kept returning to the tribe's future and the powerful vision he had experienced in the water. It had been so real, so vivid, so profoundly moving that the hand of the Great Spirit must have guided it to him.

The meaning of the vision was disturbingly clear: for the red man, there could never be peace with the white man. Arrow Keeper had foreseen in awful detail the suffering that was in store for his people. Soon, during cold moons yet to come, the Cheyenne would be forced to flee north to the Land of the Grandmother, which the whites called Canada. There, the wind would howl like mating wolves, and the temperature would fall so low the trees would split open with sounds like gunshots.

In his vision, there was no wood for fires. The only way to save some of the infants was to slaughter ponies and remove most of the guts, stuffing the little ones inside to keep them from freezing. The old people froze with the death song still on their lips.

But the vision also prophesied the rise of the long-lost son of the great chief Running Antelope—a son who had been reported killed along with his father and mother many winters earlier. That young warrior would gather his people from all their far-flung hiding places and lead the Cheyenne in one last great victory.

Arrow Keeper understood the hopeful meaning of such a vision in the autumn of his long life. His body was still straight and leather hard. But it was also gaunt and worn from making so many medicine fasts to obtain special protection for the tribe. He was worried. Soon he would be called to the Land of Ghosts, and the tribe would be left to face its most difficult times without him. The young mystery warrior would be the tribe's only hope.

As Arrow Keeper was nearing camp, his pony suddenly nickered, and the old man was instantly as alert as a wading bird. Despite his age his senses were keen. He searched the trail and the thick growth between himself and his sister the river. Sniffing the air, he listened carefully for a note of alarm in the calls of geese and crows and hawks.

He was an excellent tracker, able to read the bend of the grass and tell how recently a track had been made. But he found nothing suspicious when he swung down off his pony and bent to examine the trail. He was not even unduly alarmed when his exploring foot discovered a hidden dugout in a thicket. The hunters often cached them alongside the river.

Nonetheless, a cool feather of fear tickled the bumps of his spine. Some danger—one not foretold in his Medicine Lake vision—was lurking nearby. Some grave threat to Yellow Bear's Cheyennes was very near at hand.

Arrow Keeper rode up the gentle grassy slope from the river and approached the camp circles. He was surprised that the crier was not riding throughout camp as usual to announce his return. Then he spotted most of the tribe crowded around the council lodge. The old medicine man urged his pony from a walk to a trot when he saw a young Indian holding a knife over another.

"No!"

At Arrow Keeper's shouted command, Wolf Who Hunts Smiling froze with his blade already touching the unconscious young prisoner's scalp.

"Yellow Bear!" Arrow Keeper said, sitting his horse. His tone was respectful but disapproving. "Have I been gone a lifetime that you now kill our young men for sport?"

"He is not one of us!" Black Elk said. But the headmen silenced the hotheaded young warrior.

As Yellow Bear explained the circumstances of the stranger's capture and the decision of the council, Arrow Keeper dismounted and crossed to where Wolf Who Hunts Smiling knelt beside the supine prisoner. After the slightest hesitation, Wolf Who Hunts Smiling reluctantly edged back out of the old man's way.

Arrow Keeper crouched, stiff knee joints popping. Unobserved by the rest of the tribe, his gnarled fingers brushed back the badly singed black hair over the youth's left temple. Buried past the hairline was a mulberry-colored birthmark in the shape of an arrowhead.

The old medicine man started when he saw the traditional mark of the warrior. For it was the birthmark of the lost Cheyenne chief whose coming was foretold at Medicine Lake! For a moment, the old man studied the unconscious youth's handsome features, which the fire had blistered and singed. He hoped to find some resemblance to Running Antelope. But he had not met the great chief many times, and he could not be sure that the features before him were his.

Rising, he addressed the headmen. "Brothers, hear me! Show mercy and spare this youth."

"Why?" Yellow Bear demanded, though in truth he was relieved. "The stones have spoken."

Arrow Keeper hesitated, noticing the hate in the eyes of Black Elk, Wolf Who Hunts Smiling, and other young men as they stared at the accused spy. If he simply announced that the prisoner was their new tribal chieftain by right of birth, the young man was as good as dead.

"Brothers! I cannot yet speak words which you may put in your pockets and take away with you. Certain things have been revealed to me in a powerful medicine dream.

"Brothers! Have I not always spoken one way to you? Do not be afraid of appearing weak if you grant mercy now. The beaver is gentle and lives on bark, yet do we not respect and value him greatly?"

The headmen watched Yellow Bear for a sign, but the old chief's face remained unreadable as he tightened his red blanket around his shoulders. He, in turn, watched Black Elk, for the spy had already been granted as a peace offering to the young Cheyenne braves.

Black Elk's angry glower and his crudely sewn ear combined to give him a fearsome aspect as he stared at the spy. But despite the bloodlust in his eye, Black Elk could not forget how Arrow Keeper's big medicine had always blessed his shield and bonnet. And two winters earlier, during the Moon When the Snow Drifts Into the Tipis, had it not been Arrow Keeper who sat through the long nights, singing the sacred cure songs that saved Black Elk's younger sister from the red-speckled cough?

"Father!" he said to Arrow Keeper. "To you I will never speak in a wolf bark, but in plain words. Black Elk swears this. When I fall I will not hit the ground. My enemy will be under me.

"Father! I hate this spy. But now I will do as you wish, for everyone knows your medicine is strong and your wisdom vast like the plains."

The headmen received Black Elk's speech with approving nods. Yellow Bear too nodded his approval. But he said, "What, then, will we do with the prisoner? Banish him from our land?"

Arrow Keeper's eyes still studied the new arrival's unconscious form. His shirt was torn and soiled, his muscular chest half exposed. "Now," thought Arrow Keeper, "comes the most difficult moment. Now you will either live or die, young Cheyenne."

"If he survives his wounds, he will live with us," answered Arrow Keeper. "Though he is older than the others, he will join Wolf Who Hunts Smiling and the other young men who are training to be warriors."

His words fell on the ears of his listeners with

the force of Bluecoat canister shot. Yellow Bear saw the relieved look on Honey Eater's face and told himself again, as he looked to Black Elk, that the stranger's arrival was a bad omen.

But the young warrior had turned his back on the proceedings. He had spoken and could not change his mind like a woman. Reluctantly, he called for Wolf Who Hunts Smiling to sheathe his knife.

His young cousin obeyed. But only after vowing silently to himself that he would kill the Cheyenne who still had the stink of the whites all over him.

Chapter 7

At first, it seemed that Wolf Who Hunts Smiling had achieved revenge after all. Within two sleeps, the prisoner lay balanced on the feather-edge of death. Hunger, exhaustion, beating, and torture had so dangerously weakened the new arrival that a pitched battle between fever and chills wracked his body. His wounds and burns puffed up with infection, further weakening him.

Taking personal care of the prisoner, Arrow Keeper heaped additional buffalo robes in his own tipi, which like Yellow Bear's stood on a lone hummock separated from the clan circles. The medicine man's rare mark of favor caused angry reactions throughout the camp. But Arrow Keeper knew full well that no one else in the tribe would care for the man they thought a spy; and if the prisoner was left to fend for himself, he would never last another night.

To heal his patient's wounds, Arrow Keeper carefully filled the open gashes with tobacco and balsam sap from spruce trees. He smeared the burns with a paste made from yarrow root. The old medicine man became alarmed when the youth's stomach would retain no nourishment. It rejected even simple foods like mashed wild peas or small slices of beaver tail boiled tender. But all he could do was give his medicine and hope for the best.

Then, on the third morning following the council's judgment, Arrow Keeper lifted the flap of his tent to find a horn cup some mystery visitor had left there. It was filled with wild-bee honey, a powerful curative—and the favorite food of Chief Yellow Bear's daughter. A brief smile invading his wrinkles, the old man mixed the honey in hot yarrow tea for the semiconscious stranger. Much to his joy, the young man did not retch it back up.

For Matthew, those three days were like riding through a dense fog. Most of the time he traveled blindly, only occasionally glimpsing a landmark or feature in the billowy confusion. His mind played cat and mouse with awareness. He was vaguely aware of the rhythmic sounds of Arrow Keeper's constant chanting and his steady rattling of snake teeth in dried gourds. To the feverish youth, they sounded like noises heard through a thick wall.

Then, on the fourth morning, his eyes eased open to meet the medicine man's. He sniffed the air and smelled elk steaks cooking somewhere. The odor made his stomach growl with ravenous appetite, and when Arrow Keeper heard the rumbling, he knew the young buck would survive.

But he was still too weak to move very far from

his robes on his own power. During the day, he lay outside in the warm sunlight, growing stronger and watching the Cheyenne village go about its life. Soon he began to recognize a basic pattern in what had at first seemed chaos.

Every morning, the hunters rode out early for game while some of the older women went to dig wild turnips. The younger males often rode out later with the warriors who trained them in weapons, tracking, or horsemanship. Likewise, Honey Eater and the other young women reported daily to a lodge made of skins stretched over saplings. There, older squaws taught them the highly prized domestic arts of the tribe.

Matthew learned these things gradually from Arrow Keeper. The old medicine man knew some English, though exactly how much remained his secret. His English was stiff and halting and mixed with bastard French he had learned during his days of trading with mountain men. As he practiced the paleface tongue again, Arrow Keeper also began teaching his young charge the Cheyenne names for the parts of his body and the common objects all around him.

Arrow Keeper had already stripped Matthew of his white man's clothing and burned it. So one of the first things he taught the novice Cheyenne was how to make leggings and a breechclout out of soft kid leather. Frowning and poking his fingers so often they dripped blood, Matthew also learned to make his first pair of elk-skin moccasins by punching holes in the leather with a bone awl and split-sinew thread.

But Arrow Keeper would not allow Matthew to don his new garments before he was purified. One night, wrapped in a buffalo robe, Matthew followed Arrow Keeper to a small, isolated hut near the river. The hut consisted of elk hides draped over a willow-branch frame.

"White man's clothing leave you unclean," the medicine man said.

Arrow Keeper went inside the hut first and started a fire to heat a circle of rocks. When they finally glowed white-hot, Matthew was instructed to enter and pour cold water on them. At first, the steam was almost too hot to breathe. Then, as rivulets of sweat began to pour off him, he felt the rest of his lingering sickness ooze through his pores.

Outside, Arrow Keeper chanted and prayed the entire time. When Matthew finally emerged, glistening with sweat, the old man handed him clumps of sage and told him to rub his body down thoroughly. Then he sent Matthew for a cooling plunge in the river. Only afterward did Arrow Keeper allow him to dress in his Cheyenne clothing.

That same night Arrow Keeper taught Matthew how to build an Indian-style fire. The white men, he explained, put the centers of the logs in the flames, which was foolishly wasteful. Indians put the ends in first and pushed the logs inward as they burned, using their entire length.

As they sat before the fire, the old man reached for his clay pipe, and Matthew started to cross toward the fire to fetch him a piece of burning punk with which he could light the pipe. Before Matthew reached the fire, the old man's skinny arm shot out to stop him, his grip like iron talons.

"Never walk between Indian and fire," Arrow Keeper warned him sternly, his profile hatchet sharp in the firelight. "This say you mean to kill enemy soon! Enemy then kill you first."

And so Matthew began to learn the customs of his people. But despite his growing friendship with Arrow Keeper, the rest of the tribe ignored him. He occasionally spotted Black Elk or Wolf Who Hunts Smiling riding in and out of camp with the other braves. But they proudly refused to glance in the direction of Arrow Keeper's tipi.

However, Matthew soon realized they were not truly ignoring him. For on the first night after he began dressing like a Cheyenne, he turned back his sleeping robes to find a handful of bloody white feathers that had been stuffed beneath them.

"The young men call you coward," Arrow Keeper told him frankly. "They say Cheyenne clothing not make you Cheyenne. They say right. Soon you train with them. Then they start think some different way."

But Matthew didn't share Arrow Keeper's confidence. There were spells when he felt so lonely and scared and hated that he would have given anything to be back home in Bighorn Falls. Even being savagely beaten by Boone Wilson wasn't as awful as being tortured by vengeful Cheyennes. At those times, he would think of Hiram Steele's hard, flint-gray eyes and his gravelly voice saying, *"I mean it, boy—your kind is not welcome here."* And the memory cut him deeper than any of the Cheyenne's insults—cut him plumb to the quick of his pride as a man. All these tangled thoughts left Matthew feeling trapped between the sap and the bark.

Matthew refused to give in to his fears, however, and he worked to fit in to his new world. One of his first shaky journeys after his recovery was a trip down to the river for a bath. It was early morning, the time of grainy half-light just before the sun clears the treetops and burns the mist off the river. Because Matthew was still light-headed, his brain full of the cobwebs of sleep, he failed to notice that he had swerved toward a secluded copse formed by curved cedars that Arrow Keeper had warned him to avoid.

Although Matthew heard faint splashing sounds coming from the copse, he thought they were made by big trout breaking surface. He stripped and pushed through the line of cedars, then his breath suddenly hitched in his chest. For the cedar brake hid a perfect little clear pool that had been dug from a natural buffalo wallow. In the center of the pool, standing naked in water up to her thighs, was Honey Eater.

Just then, the sun sent its first golden shafts through the treetops, dappling the girl's supple, coltish body. Unbraided, her thick black hair fell over her breasts, which were full and heavy with dark brown nipples that thrust through her dangling tresses. She was lean and fine limbed, her wet, naked skin like glistening copper.

Only later would Matthew understand fully that the Cheyenne valued chastity and privacy more than any other Plains Indians. Unlike the Arapahoe or their Teton Sioux cousins, Cheyenne couples always placed flaps over their tipi entrances so love-making could be private. No self-respecting Cheyenne female would let a man see her naked unless they had both performed the squaw-taking ceremony.

But as their guilty eyes feasted on each other's nakedness, both Honey Eater and Matthew were powerless to move in the first shock of realization.

Then, horrified, Honey Eater ducked down until only her head was above water.

In his confusion, Matthew forgot the few Cheyenne words Arrow Keeper had taught him. "I'm sorry!" he stammered in English. But the strange language only frightened the maiden more. He turned and hurried away, his face flaming with shame—and another kind of heat burned his loins.

That night Arrow Keeper informed him tersely that they were soon to make a two-day journey to Medicine Lake. He patiently ignored the youth's questions. Instead he said, "No one with white man's name touch water of Medicine Lake and live long. Tonight Matthew must die."

The words startled the youth. Then Arrow Keeper explained that it was necessary to give him an Indian name to fool Death. He led the boy back down to the sweat lodge, where Matthew purified himself again in steam.

When he came outside, gleaming in the brilliant moonlight, Arrow Keeper had dug a small hole. The Cheyenne, like all Indians, he explained, had two names. The first was given at birth, the second earned when they were older.

"The first name your red father gave you," said Arrow Keeper, his voice barely audible above the steady purl of the river, "now lost in big wind the white man call Time. So this night I give new one. You must earn second name later, much later. But first come many trials, battles, and long trail of tears."

Arrow Keeper prayed, shook his gourd rattle, then bent close to the hole and spoke the name Matthew three times aloud. He pushed the dirt back in the hole, burying the name forever.

"Now," he declared, "white man in you gone

under forever. Never speak that name on tongue
or in heart."

"But then who am I?" The youth's voice was
almost a whisper in the moonlit darkness.

Still kneeling, Arrow Keeper looked up at the
towering youth. From that angle, he seemed almost a giant, as if his head and shoulders were
supporting the cloudy home of the Great Spirit.
Recalling his vision at Medicine Lake, Arrow
Keeper knew what to call him. He spoke the Cheyenne name. Haltingly at first, his young companion repeated it several times until it came off his
tongue easily.

"What does it mean?"

"That Matthew is dead. Tonight you join Yellow
Bear's *Shaiyena* people as he who is called Touch
the Sky!"

The Pawnee scout named Fleet Foot observed
the old man and the youth with curiosity. What,
he wondered, had caused the camp's surprising
change of heart toward their prisoner?

He stood behind a deadfall only 30 yards from
the sweat lodge, but the steady chuckle of the
nearby flowing river drowned out the words spoken by the two Cheyenne.

Fleet Foot had rubbed his shaved skull with
river mud to cut reflection from the bright moonlight. It did not matter what the old man had spoken to soften the tribe's heart toward the youth,
he thought idly as he gnawed on a strip of dried
venison. All would die soon enough—or wish they
had.

Since he had started spying on the tribe, Fleet
Foot had carefully learned the number and posi-
tioning of the night guards who watched the far-

flung pony herds. He knew all the locations where the sentries moved the horses in search of good forage. The next day, he would climb high up into the surrounding rimrock. From there, using the sun and a little shard of mirror, he would signal to the main body of warriors, who were at that very moment taking advantage of darkness to gather below the Crazy Woman Fork of the Powder for the attack.

Fleet Foot smiled grimly at the thought that not even the Great Spirit could save Yellow Bear's tribe from total destruction.

Chapter 8

Matthew was wakened early the next morning by a light touch on his shoulder. "Soon we must ride, Touch the Sky," Arrow Keeper greeted him in Cheyenne.

Hearing his new name startled him awake like a splash of cold water. The Cheyenne youth sat up, knuckling the sleep from his eyes. Arrow Keeper still had not told him why, but that day they were setting out toward the Black Hills to the southeast, home of Medicine Lake.

For breakfast, they ate elk steaks dripping kidney fat, which had been cooked on a tripod outside the tipi entrance. It was just before sunup and most of the gamblers and racers and mourners had finally settled down to sleep. Returning from his bath, Matthew saw Honey Eater and several other young women. They were heading toward the cedar brake and the women's bathing pool down-

river. Most of them watched him with open
interest, a few even smiling. Honey Eater, however, coldly averted her gaze. Matthew recalled
their accidental meeting at the pool and felt heat
rising to his face. From her actions, he could tell
that she believed he had deliberately spied on her
as she bathed.

Although Matthew was upset by Honey Eater's
reaction, Arrow Keeper left him no time to brood
about the maiden for they had much to do before
departing. First they filled legging sashes with
chunks of venison, jerked buffalo, and dried fruit.
Then they walked to the pony corral. Arrow
Keeper singled out his usual piebald and a handsome dun with a white blaze on its forehead. He
handed the dun's hair bridle to Matthew.

"This one know tricks," he said in English.

"What kind of tricks?"

But the old medicine man ignored him as he
folded a blanket over his piebald. Matthew followed suit, hoping he would be quick to get the
knack of riding bareback. For War Bonnet had
given away his saddle along with everything else
Matthew had brought with him, and he wouldn't
have a chance to get another.

By the time they were ready, cooking smoke
curled out of the tops of most tipis. Arrow Keeper
returned to his own tipi and carefully removed a
coyote-fur bag hidden under his sleeping robes.
Seeing Matthew eye the bag curiously, he opened
it. Four stone-tipped arrows dyed bright blue and
yellow and fletched with scarlet feathers lay inside.

"The sacred Medicine Arrows," the old man told
him proudly. "If this village is attacked, I protect
the arrows with my life. Because of this great

71

honor, I am Arrow Keeper and I lead the Medicine Arrows ceremony."

The fate of the four arrows, he added, represented the fate of the tribe. If the medicine arrows were lost or bloodied, the same fate would befall the tribe.

After leaving the arrows with Medicine Bottle for safekeeping, they pointed their mounts toward the Black Hills in the southeast. For the first few hours, Arrow Keeper spoke only occasionally. The land at first was mostly open plains and short-grass prairie. Once Arrow Keeper stopped alongside a creek to point out a floater stick that marked an Indian beaver trap below. In the higher country, he taught Matthew to recognize and name marigold, columbine, mountain laurel, the leathery leaves of myrtle—all of which had their uses as food or medicine.

The longer they rode, the more the boy's legs ached from gripping the pony's flanks with his knees, and his backside grew sore from constant jarring. But he was getting better at sensing the spirited dun's rhythm and riding with the motion instead of against it.

Matthew noticed that Arrow Keeper constantly kept his eyes on the sparrow hawks overhead, occasionally frowning. Toward midday they rode across a dried-up riverbed, its parched mud webbed with cracks. Suddenly, Arrow Keeper turned his piebald around in the direction of Yellow Bear's camp. Many minutes passed while he sat still and quiet, as if listening for something.

"What is it?" the youth said nervously.

The old man's hawklike profile remained impassive. Finally he looked at the boy and said, "Nothing. It was only *odjib*."

"*Odjib*, Father?"

"A thing of smoke, a memory smell. Nothing real."

But Arrow Keeper's brow was still furrowed with worry as they rode on. Not until they stopped in the shade of a huge cottonwood to eat did Arrow Keeper finally begin to speak more than a few terse words. He talked less and less in English, switching to it only when Matthew did not understand him.

He told Matthew about their brothers the Southern Cheyenne, who would soon come north for the summer medicine ceremonies. They lived below the Arkansas River with the Southern Arapahoe, the Kiowa, and the bloodthirsty Comanche. The Northern Cheyenne's nearby cousins were the Teton Sioux, who were such close battle allies that some had been permitted to join Yellow Bear's tribe by marriage or rite. The Cheyenne's sworn Indian enemies included the Crow, the turncoat Ute, and the treacherous Pawnee.

"Understand this well," Arrow Keeper said. "The Pawnee is cunning like the fox. He will raise one hand in friendship while the other draws a weapon to kill you."

The two rode on again after the ponies had grazed and drunk their fill from a streamlet. By the time their shadows were long in the sun, they had reached the grassy tableland of the Little Missouri River, which marked the halfway point between Yellow Bear's camp and the western edge of the Black Hills.

Arrow Keeper halted and removed eight small, tough pieces of hide from his sash. He handed four to Matthew. "Tie these around your pony's hooves."

"Why, Father?"

"Because ponies need moccasins too if they wish to move silently."

The youth understood the need for silence when they reached the top of the next wooded crest. Below, in the lush green valley of the Little Missouri, a new fort was partially built. The outer walls were made of thick cottonwood, the loopholed buildings inside of pine log. Several companies of infantry and horse soldiers were camped in outlying ranks of tents. Huge wagon-mounted guns were aimed at the very crest where they rode, ready to cut down attackers with screaming bits of shrapnel.

"The Bluecoats are more dangerous than even the Pawnee," Arrow Keeper told his companion in a hushed voice. "The Bluecoats are strong and they wish to destroy all red men. Ride quietly now and stay behind trees. Pony soldiers may be anywhere."

The two Cheyenne kept below the ridge for a while. When they were well past the fort, a red fox abruptly streaked across the trail in front of the dun pony's forelegs, startling her. She nickered, shied, and bolted sideways toward the crest of the ridge. Matthew barely managed to purchase a good grip in time to avoid being thrown. But by the time he had the pony under control, they had broken through the treeline into full view of a Bluecoat squad.

Some of the soldiers were gathered around a mule-drawn flatbed wagon. They had been hauling logs back to the fort when the work detail got caught in a sudden downpour. As a result, the wagon was mired up to its axles in mud.

There was a shout of alarm when the horse-mounted guards spotted Matthew. Lead balls whizzed past his ears as he urged the dun around to join Arrow Keeper back behind the treeline. But he could hear the sudden thudding of shod hooves behind him, and he knew the soldiers were giving pursuit. Fear dropped like a cold ball of ice into his stomach.

Matthew leaned low over the dun's neck, urging her on. She leaped a fallen log and then he could glimpse Arrow Keeper's pony ahead through the trees, already warned into flight by the carbine shots. More lead balls flew past his ears so closely they sounded like angry bumblebees. The soldiers were near enough behind him that Matthew could hear them cursing.

A booming report exploded as a soldier fired a double load of buckshot from a scattergun. Most of the pellets fell short, but Matthew felt a dozen fiery antbites on his bare back. The dun caught a few pellets too and surged forward.

Arrow Keeper had no magic for being invisible that would work for the uninitiated youth. Once or twice, he glanced behind to make sure the boy was staying close. He led them along a narrow, overgrown trail, branches swiping at their faces as they flew past. But their ponies were tired and their pursuers dogged.

Quickly the Cheyenne ponies were lathered, sides heaving. If Arrow Keeper didn't act quickly, their lives would be forfeit. Just after the trail made a sharp dogleg turn to avoid a bluff, Arrow Keeper abruptly halted his mount and swung down. He signaled the youth to do the same.

Matthew could taste fear in his throat. He heard the soldiers closing in behind them, about to make the sharp turn and spot them. But Arrow Keeper made it clear then why he had selected those particular ponies. He led both animals about ten yards away from the trail. Then he snorted once loudly as a horse does when clearing its nostrils after drinking.

Matthew's jaw dropped open in astonishment when both ponies obediently lay flat on their sides, heads down. With their mounts almost out of sight in the low but dense undergrowth, the two Cheyenne flattened themselves down behind their ponies.

Three or four riders passed in a loud, fast thudding of hooves, then the noise grew dimmer until it disappeared.

Since the day was late and their mounts exhausted, Arrow Keeper chose not to risk going on and meeting the returning patrol. Instead, they moved back even farther from the trail and made camp for the night. Later, under cover of the darkness, they led their horses back out to open grass, where they could be left on long tethers to graze. On their way back to camp they discovered a small cave, and they decided they could risk a fire within it.

His features sharply etched in the flickering firelight, Arrow Keeper picked a few pellets from the boy's back with a bone-handle knife.

"There is much white man's foolishness which you must forget," he said while he worked. "Such as this fire."

"But, Father! I built it Indian fashion just as you showed me."

"True. But see how much green oak you used? See how it throws off sparks? Many foolish whites have burned in their blankets from flying sparks."

They spoke thus long into the night, and Arrow

Keeper explained how to measure time in sleeps, moons, and winters instead of days, months, and years.

"What about hours and minutes and seconds?"

Arrow Keeper frowned at the unfamiliar English words. "What are these things?"

He listened carefully as Matthew tried to explain. Then he replied simply: "These things do not exist for Indians. They were buried in that hole along with your white name."

Late on the second day, they reached the dark, forested humps of the Black Hills. It was well past sundown by the time they tethered their ponies on the isolated shores of the high-altitude lake the Cheyenne called Medicine Lake.

Matthew noticed a change in the old man's manner. His tone was more hushed there, more reverential. That night they stared into the fire and listened to the eerie cry of loons out on the moonlit lake. Arrow Keeper told his companion many important lessons could be learned there at the center of the Indian world.

"This is the place of gods and holy mountains, not just for the *Shaiyena*, but for all red men of the plains. But now gold-hungry white men are invading. They are driving the red man farther and farther west from this sacred place, farther from our buffalo herds.

"The white man says, 'You must be like us and raise cows and corn. If not, we kill you off like the buffalo.' But the Indian and the buffalo are one, and they will die together!"

Solemnly, the old man explained that no Cheyenne could cross over to the Land of Ghosts unless he had sung the Death Song in the moments before dying. His voice hushed and cracking with age, he chanted the simple words that Matthew must never himself sing until death was inevitable:

Nothing lives long
Only the earth and the mountains.

The words had a sad, yet dignified and peaceful ring as they echoed in the darkness out over the water. Then, the spiritual lesson complete, Arrow Keeper removed a soft kid pouch from his sash and handed it to the youth.

Arrow Keeper was almost convinced now that the youth was the son of the great Northern Cheyenne chief Running Antelope. Running Antelope's medicine sign had been the ferocious badger, and the pouch Arrow Keeper gave Matthew contained a set of sharp badger claws. But the old man would not yet tell the boy who he really was. The time had not yet come.

"Your medicine bag," Arrow Keeper explained simply. "Wear it always. Protect it with your life. An enemy who steals your medicine bag steals your soul. Better he should scalp you."

Matthew tied the bag to his breechclout with a buckskin thong, and Arrow Keeper fell into a deep, reflective silence. When the boy started to ask what they would be doing the next day, Arrow Keeper silenced him.

"No more talk now. You will need strength for tomorrow." The old man pointed to his ears, his eyes, and his nose. "True it is, old men talk too much. Sometimes talking puts a brave in trouble. More can be learned from the talk without words. Listen to your mother the earth."

Matthew slept deeply that night. He woke at sunrise to the glorious singing of meadowlarks and hermit thrushes, grosbeaks and warbling orioles. In the morning light, he saw how beautiful the small mountain lake was, its placid blue surface wrinkling in the wind.

But even before he could bathe or eat, Arrow Keeper led him around to a small hill at the opposite end of the lake.

"You tell me, 'Arrow Keeper, I will be a Cheyenne.' But have you taken this desire close to your heart and thought what it means? This day, we will see if you can ever be a true Cheyenne in mind and spirit. As proof of your desire to join Yellow Bear's people, you must stand on this hill with your eyes shut until sunset. You must not move a muscle except to keep your face always turned directly into the sun."

His words spoken, the old man left Matthew there alone. At first, Matthew was only mildly annoyed with the order. Still, it shouldn't be to hard to stand on the hill all day with his eyes squeezed shut.

But before an hour had passed, he was miserable. His legs ached, and his belly constantly growled for nourishment. Even with his eyes closed, the bright sunlight made them tremble and water. As the morning progressed, the sun blazed warmer and warmer. Soon rivulets of sweat flowed freely down his scalp.

By midday, he was sure he would fail. Even his dark skin, which had never burned, was starting to sting from the unrelenting exposure. As his thirst increased, he grew lightheaded, occasionally swaying as if he would drop. In his confusion, he forgot where he was. He heard his ma and pa and Corey and Old Knobby and Kristen, all begging him to come home, begging him to—

He swayed, catching himself just before he fell.

From the heat of the sun, he guessed it had sunk low over the western edge of the lake perhaps only an hour from setting. But Matthew could endure no more.

Suddenly, Arrow Keeper was at Matthew's side, his voice startling the youth after the long silence. "As the twig is bent, so the tree shall grow. If you cannot endure this small thing here today, how will you stand and fight when the war cry sounds? When the blood of your people stains the earth?"

The words rallied Matthew and touched something deep inside. His mouth formed a grim, determined slit, muscles bunched around his clenched jaws. He was still there, legs trembling but upright, when the sun finally dipped below the horizon and Arrow Keeper touched his shoulder.

"Now," the old man told him, pride clear in his tone, "you have begun to be a Cheyenne."

So stiff he limped, the exhausted youth bathed quickly. He fell into a deep, dreamless sleep while he was still chewing a hunk of venison. Hours later, he was startled awake by a strangled cry from Arrow Keeper.

The old man had experienced a powerful medicine dream. His face ghastly in the glow of the dying embers, old and lined beyond his years, Arrow Keeper rose quickly from his buffalo robe and spoke urgently to his companion.

"Prepare to ride. Yellow Bear's camp is burning!"

Chapter 9

The moon was halfway through her journey across the night sky, but still Honey Eater could not sleep. She lay quietly in her robes and listened to the nighttime noises outside in the camp. Closer at hand, on the other side of the center pole of her father's tipi, Yellow Bear and her mother Singing Woman were sound asleep, oblivious to their daughter's restlessness.

From down near the river came an owl hoot. Honey Eater heard it and idly wondered at it. Usually owls did not hunt so close to the camp. But her mind soon lost that thought and turned once again to the new arrival. Where had Arrow Keeper and he gone to when they rode away two sleeps earlier?

Thinking about him so much bothered Honey Eater. She was, after all, the daughter of a chief. He was only a pathetic outcast who looked Indian but acted white. She knew it angered her father to see her gazing at the stranger so often. But something about the tall, broad-shouldered youth was different—something besides his stature and pleasing looks. He was somehow marked for something great.

The young maiden had seen it when he was lashed to the wagon wheel and tortured over embers. Despite his shocking ignorance and white man's contamination, he was strong and brave and good in a way that showed in his eyes, in the determined set of his mouth.

Her face flushing with warmth, she recalled their embarrassing encounter at the bathing pool. At first, she had believed he spied on her; now she realized he had simply blundered upon her in his ignorance. But still, they were not married and had seen each other naked! She could hardly be expected to be friendly toward him after such a breach of custom and still call herself a modest Cheyenne maiden. And why was a modest Cheyenne maiden, she scolded herself, thinking so often about how magnificent he had looked naked?

She lost her thoughts when another owl hooted, even closer than the last. Nearby, yet another owl replied, almost as if signaling. Honey Eater frowned. A sudden premonition of danger moved up her spine in a cool tickle. She slipped her buckskin dress over her slim shoulders and silently lifted the hide flap over the tipi's entrance.

Moonlight limned the camp in a silver-white glow like brittle frost. From her family's tipi, which sat on a lone hummock between the river and the rest of camp, she could see the dark mass of trees on the riverbank, the cone-shaped tipis, the darker, larger masses of the lodges. All was quiet and peaceful.

She was about to lower the flap and return to her robes when the night sky suddenly rained fire. It started with one lone orange streak that arced across the sky from the direction of the trees behind the corral. At first, she thought it was a brilliant falling star, one that came closer to the camp than most. Then she heard the hard, familiar *thwap* of an arrowhead embedding itself in a target. A moment later, the council lodge was in flames, and more fire was raining down on the camp. Flaming arrows whipped past overhead by the dozens, lodging in tipis, panicking ponies, lighting the entire camp in a strange orange glow.

Honey Eater screamed at the same moment a surprised sentry sounded the wolf howl of danger, shattering the quiet. Horses nickered in fright and crashed through the corral in a thunder of hooves; braves, many still naked, stumbled from their tipis. Their first priority, even before they knew who their attackers were, was to form a line of defense so the women, children, and elders could escape.

As the enemy poured out from the trees in the eerie firelight, Honey Eater recognized the dreaded Pawnee! Her heart skipped a beat. All Cheyenne women knew full well what these evil, cricket-eating marauders did to female captives.

Gunfire and shouting rang out with deafening intensity. Yellow Bear had already stumbled past his daughter to direct the warriors. When Singing Woman ran out, still wrapping her blanket, she grasped her daughter's arm and started to lead her toward the others fleeing to a prearranged escape route downriver.

The next moment, her mother stumbled to one side as if she'd been violently tugged. Then she dropped like a stone, blood pumping in thick jets where a lead ball had just shattered her skull.

Watching her mother die before her eyes shocked Honey Eater into immobility. She stood rooted, even though the Pawnee were entering the camp, the firelight reflecting blood in their wild eyes. Their faces and shaved skulls were painted vermillion and ocher, their bodies smudged with ashes. They had been made brave and reckless by drinking the white man's strong water. The kind the Pawnee warriors liked was traded from the unlicensed whites who added things to the devil water—things that made the Indians even crazier when drunk.

And they were surely crazy that night, Honey Eater saw from their fierce and relentless attack. Armed with bows, lances, clubs, knives, battle-axes, and tomahawks, the Pawnee cut down everything in their path.

The Cheyenne warriors—and even some boys and old men—met the attack bravely. No Cheyenne ever expected to survive if he were attacked before he could dress and paint and make an offering to the sacred Medicine Arrows. Yet, with only death to look forward to, they held fast to save the tribe.

Yellow Bear, his white hair flying like a mane, grabbed the lance of a fallen warrior. He tried to run forward. But two elderly headmen, knowing chaos would descend on the tribe if he were killed, restrained him. They forced him to retreat with them toward the escape trail, gathering children along the way.

Dead ponies lay everywhere, and Cheyenne

braves used them as breastworks to stem the attack. While Honey Eater watched the squirmish, War Bonnet stood up to throw his lance at an attacker. But before the lance could leave his hand, a double-bladed throwing axe opened up War Bonnet's chest and dropped him in his tracks, a bloody geyser spouting from his breastbone.

Abruptly the fierce Cheyenne war cry sounded close in her ears. *"Hiya hi-i-i-ya!"* And the warrior called Black Elk led a counter charge. He leaped toward a Pawnee brave, cracking him over the head with his lance to count first coup before he killed his enemy. Black Elk was fierce and magnificent in his wrath, and his counter attack roused his brothers to heroic deeds. As the Pawnee fell, young Cheyenne boys bravely darted forward to snatch up their weapons.

As the entire camp blazed with an eerie ghost-light, old Medicine Bottle picked up a crying child, then grabbed the stunned girl's hand and led her toward the river escape point. Buffalo-hide rafts had been stashed in the event of an attack. The elders and the smallest children were being floated across by young boys big enough to swim.

But while he fled with Honey Eater and the child, Medicine Bottle took an arrow flush through the neck and fell, dropping the child. Finally prodded back into action by the old man's sacrifice, Honey Eater sprang forward and scooped the infant into her arms. She ran toward the river as the Cheyenne braves waged a retreating battle all around her.

No rafts were available when she reached the bank of the Powder. Wolf Who Hunts Smiling was armed with the Colt rifle that he had taken from the newcomer. He had been ordered to protect the

Judd Cole

river escape route with his life. But with all his heart, he yearned to prove himself in the main battle.

Children who had just seen their parents killed stood naked and wailing, and old grandmothers tried to comfort them. Honey Eater held the child close to her breast, and the image of her own mother falling dead raced through her mind.

The river was swollen and fast from the spring melt. On the opposite shore, two boys were desperately unloading a raft so they could guide it back across. But Honey Eater glanced at the horrible scene behind her and realized that the Pawnee attackers were getting closer. If they reached the river, Wolf Who Hunts Smiling could never stop all of them.

In the middle of the camp, one of the Pawnee held a young, screaming Cheyenne woman down while another savagely raped her. Honey Eater recognized the girl as Morning Star of the Eagle clan, who had often served with her as a maid of honor for the Sun Dance ceremony. When the Pawnee's lust was sated, he gutted her with his knife.

At Honey Eater's side, an old woman named Rain Necklace said to her, "Prepare yourself for the Land of Ghosts, little daughter!" Then she began chanting the Death Song.

Despite the danger pressing closer, Honey Eater could not bring herself to chant the final words of her life. Instead, she tugged at a thong around her neck, pulling a small knife out from under her dress. All Cheyenne women wore one just like it night and day. It would be used to kill the child and herself if capture seemed inevitable.

"Prepare yourself to die, little daughter!" the old grandmother urged her again.

Honey Eater tasted the squalling infant's tears even as she tightened her grip on the knife.

Arrow Keeper and Matthew rode hard without stopping to sleep. Eating while they rode, they paused only briefly to rest and water the horses. Once they were forced to shelter in the lee of a mesa during a brief but violent windstorm. They made the return to Yellow Bear's camp in half the time they had taken to make the journey to Medicine Lake.

But Yellow Bear's camp was no longer recognizable. Most of the tipis and lodges lay in blackened ruins. The ponies that weren't missing from the ruined corrals lay dead everywhere, already bloating and starting to draw dark swarms of flies. The camp was terrifying and heartrending. Wailing over their dead braves, squaws sat bloodied from gouging themselves with sharp flints. All of the surviving warriors had cut short their hair for the dead. Those suffering extreme grief had gashed themselves with knives until blood streamed freely from the wounds.

His voice as sad as his eyes, Yellow Bear described the raid to Arrow Keeper. The outcome would have been even worse, the old chief assured him, if a Sioux hunting party had not been camped nearby. Hearing the battle sounds, they rode in and scattered the surprised Pawnee.

Matthew stood rooted in the middle of camp. He was overwhelmed by the suffering and death surrounding him. Since the raid, the dead had been washed and dressed in new moccasins for their journey to the Land of Ghosts. But not all the screams came from mourners. A Pawnee prisoner was lashed to the same wagon wheel he recognized from his own torture session. Embers glowed beneath the Pawnee, and the sickly sweet stink of scorched flesh filled the camp. Nearby, another prisoner sat lashed to a tree. He was just conscious enough to watch ravenous dogs feed on the warm intestines that had been pulled through the slit in his gut.

His heart thudding loudly in his ears, Matthew wandered the devastated camp until he spotted Honey Eater. She was helping an old squaw prepare Singing Woman's body. It had already been washed and wrapped in deerskin and soon would be hauled to its burial scaffold. Once high in place, she would be wrapped tightly in buffalo skins.

Matthew's gaze met Honey Eater's long enough to give him a sharp pang of pity and sorrow at the grief in her eyes. But mixed with that feeling was a glimmer of hope. For he could see that she was relieved to see him alive again.

When Matthew turned away, he ran into Black Elk, who had witnessed their exchange of glances. The jealous young brave scowled fiercely at him. Then he approached the group of headmen and braves gathered around the Chief and Arrow Keeper.

"Fathers! Brothers! Hear me well! When did Black Elk ever show the white feather to an enemy? Did he ever hide in his tipi while his brothers were on the warpath? No! Count his scalps, count his war feathers! Black Elk swears the scalps of those who did these things will hang on our lodgepoles."

Yellow Bear heard Black Elk's words in silence. Then he turned to Arrow Keeper. The old chief's eyes were sad with a grief too great to express. He too had hacked off his hair.

"Was not Singing Woman the soul of my medicine bag? Twice now have I lost good wives to my enemies. I have fought on the plains and on the icy slopes of the Wolf Mountains. Long now have I sung the songs of peace like the friendly Ponca. Long now have I counseled my young men not to dance the war dance. But from this time forward my heart is a stone. There is no soft spot left in it!"

"I have ears for this talk," Black Elk approved, his dark eyes fierce. Again Matthew stared in gruesome fascination at the angry, crooked scar where Black Elk's ear had been sewn back on. "Yellow Bear speaks of the peaceful Ponca. Do they not raise corn and gardens and cows? And yet, are they not constantly raided and attacked just as we were attacked here? Women live in peace and grow gardens. True braves hunt and fight. Give me warriors, Father, and I will avenge Yellow Bear's people."

Yellow Bear met Black Elk's declaration with a silent nod. Unfortunately, he knew, revenge would be a difficult matter. Cheyenne trackers reported that the fleeing Pawnee had cleverly stuck to a buffalo run, where their tracks would be obscured by stampeding herds. Even more discouraging was the fact that precious few braves were left in the Cheyenne tribe.

"Yellow Bear cannot give Black Elk warriors," the old chief finally said. "Instead of tall trees, I have only acorns."

Yellow Bear's tired eyes prowled the devastated camp as if painting a memory for eternity. For a moment, his eyes lingered on young Wolf Who Hunts Smiling, who stood near his cousin Black Elk.

89

Then Matthew was startled when the tribe leader's gaze fell on him. "I have only acorns," he repeated. "But acorns become trees. Black Elk will take charge of all the bucks who have twelve winters or more, but are not yet blooded warriors. He will train them well and quickly. For until he does so, our clan circles are unprotected."

Black Elk's eyes showed a fierce but dignified pride when he received the important order. But he too glanced again at Matthew. It had not escaped his notice that the newcomer's arrival had been suspiciously close to the time of the attack. Could the spy have left secret messages for the Pawnee in the forks of nearby trees?

"All the bucks?" Black Elk demanded, scowling at Matthew.

Arrow Keeper gave a determined nod to the chief. "All," Yellow Bear said.

Black Elk exchanged a secret, knowing glance with his young cousin. Both then stared hard at Matthew.

"As you say, Father," said Black Elk. "But perhaps not all will survive the hard training."

Chapter 10

Soon the last bodies were placed on scaffolds deep in the forest. With the mournful sound of chanting in the background, the surviving headmen met in outdoor council with Yellow Bear and Arrow Keeper. Although the sacred Medicine Arrows had not been harmed when Medicine Bottle's tipi burned, the men of the tribe unanimously agreed that too much death had left bad medicine at their present camp.

In the Moon When the Green Grass Is Up, Yellow Bear's tribe moved west and resettled in the Tongue River valley. They selected a vast, grassy site halfway between the Powder and the Rosebud and just north of the Bighorn Mountains. Since the new camp was in wild mustang country, the tribe quickly began to gather a new pony herd.

Matthew and old Arrow Keeper hacked short their hair like the others, cropping it unevenly with sharp skinning knives. But Matthew's gesture of sympathy was scorned by Black Elk, Wolf Who Hunts Smiling, and many braves who still mistrusted him.

The warrior training began in earnest after the tribe's move. Black Elk divided the youths into several groups of five, assigning a full warrior to take charge of each group. He himself took charge of his cousin Wolf Who Hunts Smiling, Matthew, a small, quiet boy named Little Horse, and twin brothers named Swift Canoe and True Son.

From the beginning, Matthew was mercilessly humiliated and scorned. Within his hearing, the others refused to call each other by name, which meant they thought he was no better than a white man. Wolf Who Hunts Smiling also refused to call him by the Cheyenne name Arrow Keeper had given him. Instead, he contemptuously called him White Man's Shoes or How-Do-You-Do, referring to the way he had greeted War Bonnet on the day he was taken prisoner. In uglier moods, Wolf Who Hunts Smiling called him Woman Face, because occasionally Matthew still let fear or other emotions show.

Though he was older than the others, Matthew was painfully aware that he was by far the most ignorant and useless. He was treated as a menial servant by Black Elk. He was ordered to keep the skins filled with fresh river water, to gather wood, to build and tend the fires, and to stand watch more often than the others. He received the same bits of meat fed to dogs back in camp and was forced to ride behind the others, choking on their dust. He was even ordered to make bullets, which was considered woman's work back at the Tongue River camp.

Swift Canoe and True Son feared and admired Wolf Who Hunts Smiling. They quickly became his surly imitators. But Little Horse, whose medicine sign was the bloodstone, was more reserved around Wolf Who Hunts Smiling. Unlike the others, he was quiet, never boastful. Perhaps, thought Matthew, he was modest because he was smaller than the other boys. But he was swift and sure in his movements, with the staying power of a fresh, strong pony. And unlike the others, he was not a complainer.

Although Little Horse quietly refused to join in the constant harassment and humiliation of Matthew, he would not meet the tall stranger's eye or offer a sign of friendship. To him, Matthew was an embarrassment. It was best to simply pretend he did not exist.

Black Elk did not respect—or trust—Matthew enough to permit him to carry his own weapons. Only his respect for Arrow Keeper's magic prevented him from letting Wolf Who Hunts Smiling murder the spy, which was, after all, the council's original decision. So only when actually practicing movements and techniques for battle, would the intruder briefly handle weapons. One day Black Elk saw Matthew staring at the rifle that had once been his. Wolf Who Hunts Smiling caught him and laughed, daring him to try to get it back.

Occasionally, when they were well away from the main camp, Black Elk's little band would harass small details of soldiers guarding wagons on their way to nearby Soldier Towns. After these practice forays, Black Elk and Wolf Who Hunts Smiling would berate Matthew mercilessly. The newcomer had learned the basic art of riding bareback. But he could not freely gallop the spirited dun Arrow Keeper had given him. Nor could he perform any of the riding stunts the others had mastered.

Clinging low to his black pony's neck, Wolf Who Hunts Smiling could rapidly swing his body from side to side at a full gallop. He could also lean down low to scoop up fallen comrades or weapons without breaking stride. When Matthew attempted such tricks, he ended up on the ground, stunned and humiliated.

Matthew suffered the same burning embarrassment when practicing shooting arrows at a gallop. Black Elk had shown the younger Indians how to charge in full battle style with lances up, bows strung, and rifles at the ready. A good Cheyenne warrior, boasted Black Elk, could string and launch ten arrows in the time it took a Bluecoat to fire and reload a carbine.

Matthew had noticed back in camp how little Cheyenne boys often played war with miniature bows and arrows. He, in contrast, had never handled a bow in his life and was all thumbs at first. He could not fit the tri-feathered arrows tipped with inch-long flint heads chipped to fine points into the bow quickly—not while also concentrating on his galloping pony. If he did manage to launch one, it always flew wide of the target.

There seemed no end to his abysmal ignorance. One evening in camp, Black Elk handed him a whetstone and a knife, its handle carved from the leg bone of an elk. He ordered him to hone the blade until it would slice hard leather. Matthew was determined to do a good job. But one side of the knife was dull beyond belief. He worked for hours, late into the night beside the dying embers, sharpening both sides of the blade to a deadly edge.

The next morning, Black Elk threw the ruined weapon into a stream. Even a rabbit, he raged, had brains enough to know that Indians sharpened their knives on one edge only!

Countless such mistakes made Matthew realize his foolishness and deeply regret not listening to old Knobby's warnings back in Bighorn Falls. But there were rare moments when the rest of Black Elk's little band simply ignored the outsider, and he could perfect his new skills without fear of being ridiculed.

Some nights, the young Indians gambled on wrestling matches, wagering with the bright beads they prized so highly. Other times, they talked and told stories for hours, and because Matthew was understanding more and more of the language, he could listen and learn. Black Elk described famous tribal battles and heroes. He told of the Cheyenne's desperate flight west when driven from their original homeland in Minnesota. At times, Black Elk told them, their people were forced to eat dead horses and dig in the sand for water.

During these sessions, Black Elk would boast not only about destroying the Pawnee, but about how easily the Cheyenne would drive the white man out. Then Matthew would realize with great wonder that the Indians had no concept of the white man's actual numbers back east.

When meat ran low, the warriors in training did not bother to ride back to the main camp on the Tongue. Instead, Black Elk led them to a lush grassland between the forks of the creeks the whites called Little Piney and Big Piney. Close to the pine-clad slopes of the Bighorns, the hunting was excellent.

Black Elk taught his charges how to attract game merely by tying a bright cloth to a stick. They lay beside it in the tall grass less than an hour before Matthew recognized the large jackass ears of a mule deer. The curious buck was moving steadily closer to investigate the cloth.

After he shot the deer, Black Elk showed the young Cheyenne how to slit it open from throat to rump. He cut away all the choice parts, including the liver, loins, kidney fat, and upper parts of the hams. That night everyone except Matthew feasted. The leftover meat was hung high in a tree to protect it.

Permitted only the stringy thigh meat, Matthew ate apart from the others as usual. His stomach rumbled at the smell of the sizzling loin steaks cooking in kidney fat. That night all he could think of besides hunger was his family and Kristen. His misery was complete.

Quietly, unobserved by the others in the dark, Little Horse walked past Matthew's robe as if on his way to make water beyond camp. But Matthew felt something land in his lap. He reached down and found a succulent chunk of loin. He ate it greedily. The next day, he tried to thank Little Horse, but the youth turned his face away before the others could see.

Occasionally during their hunting trips, Black Elk would carve signs on the bark of trees that would direct hunters who came after them to hidden salt licks or streams where game was rich.

While leaving the Bighorn hunting grounds, they spotted a Sioux hunting party on a nearby ridge. The Sioux raised their lances high overhead in greeting. Though the main body rode on, they sent a word-bringer riding down to meet their Cheyenne cousins.

The Sioux wore a captured Bluecoat blouse, and his hair was braided and wrapped around his head. A message from any red brother was always an important thing, Black Elk assured his younger charges. Therefore the word-bringer was greeted warmly, fed, and given tobacco to fill his clay pipe. Only after he and Black Elk had smoked to the four directions did the Sioux messenger deliver his speech.

First he presented Black Elk a chamois pouch filled with choice white man's tobacco. Then he spoke in the curious mixture of Cheyenne and Sioux, which both tribes had come to understand.

"A gift from Chief Spring Dance of the Lakota people. We have heard of the tragedy at Yellow Bear's camp on the Powder. We have fasted for three sleeps, crying in our hearts for our red brothers.

"During the Snowblind Moon, when death stalked the Lakota people like a hungry wolf, it was Yellow Bear's Cheyenne who gave us pemmican. The enemy of the Cheyenne is the enemy of the Lakota, and we will raise our battle lances beside yours!"

Such talk ignited approving fire in the eyes of Black Elk and Wolf Who Hunts Smiling. It was Sioux bravery, after all, that had saved Yellow Bear's village from total destruction. Despite the way he was being treated, Matthew too felt himself caught up in the tribe's urgent need to punish their Pawnee attackers. For he knew he could never forget the sorrow and horror in Honey Eater's eyes as she prepared her dead mother for the final journey.

Sometimes, in rare moments by himself, Matthew actually forgot his misery briefly. It might happen early in the morning, when the grass was still wet with dew and the sun newly risen on the horizon. While the others slept, he would lead the dun in practice gallops. Then, riding freely, his face into the cool wind, it was easy to remember Arrow Keeper's advice to rely less on talking and thinking and more on his other senses.

Such moments, however, were few and far between. His sworn enemy Wolf Who Hunts Smiling was relentless in making his existence wretched. Though he feared the ferocious Black Elk, Matthew sensed it was Wolf Who Hunts Smiling he must fear most. The young hothead's sharp-featured, wily face befitted his name. His eyes were as swift as minnows and missed nothing. He was large for his age and showed a brash, sometimes even reckless, courage of which Black Elk approved.

Back at the Tongue River camp, Matthew had noticed how the blooded warriors showed a certain dignified restraint around the women and children. It was their way to keep their eyes straight ahead and appear uninterested in the proceedings around them. After all, they had trod the warpath. Wolf Who Hunts Smiling aped their mannerisms. He avoided the youths who were his own age and tagged after Black Elk and the other braves.

Early one morning, Black Elk instructed his group in the important skill of throwing a tomahawk from horseback. Three times he rode past a cottonwood at full gallop. Each time he leaned far off his horse and sent the tomahawk flying with deadly accuracy. After his final throw, it took both Swift Canoe and his brother True Son together to pull the embedded tomahawk free of the rough bark.

Then it was time for the others to try their skill. Little Horse rode first, barely missing on his first two passes, but hitting solidly on the third. Swift Canoe and True Son did nearly as well. Wolf Who Hunts Smiling, however, sank the blade two inches into the wood on his first pass.

"Now," Black Elk said, "let us see how Woman Face would cut down a Pawnee!"

His face flaming at the insulting name, Matthew accepted the tomahawk and wheeled his dun around. He paced off the approach as the others had, then turned his pony again. The others sat their horses 20 paces back from the cottonwood, watching him with cold scorn.

Nervous sweat beaded in his unevenly cropped hair like crawling insects. Matthew nudged the spirited pony's flanks with his heels. A moment later, he was flying at a full gallop, bearing down on the tree. He knew the throw was wrong even before he finished it. Not only did he miss the tree completely, but the tomahawk bounced sloppily off a second tree and ricocheted back across his path. Quicker than the blink of an eye, it struck his own pony in the right flank, cutting her.

It was not a serious injury, but the awful significance of his blunder wiped the amused jeers off the faces of the others. Their hateful, mocking stares said clearly that a pony warrior who carelessly injured his own mount was beneath contempt—on a level with the stupid white men who would ruin a horse's flanks with sharp-roweled spurs!

That night, to punish him, Black Elk assigned Matthew to a double watch. Night sentries were always necessary because most Indians slept soundly—so soundly that, on important occasions such as nights before battle, they drank great amounts of water so their aching bladders would wake them early.

As he stood his watch, Matthew hoped for no trouble, but that day's humiliation was still not complete. A few sleeps earlier the young Cheyenne had encountered another group of Cheyenne from a camp on the Rosebud. Both groups had gambled on pony races, and Swift Canoe and True Son had won a calico shawl as a present for their mother Gentle Wind. That night, as Matthew knelt beside the fire to tend it, Wolf Who Hunts Smiling rose quietly behind him. A moment later, Matthew felt a light weight drape itself over his shoulders, and suddenly everyone in camp, except Little Horse, howled with derisive laughter.

Matthew stood back up, his face flaming with shame as he pulled the shawl off and threw it down. Among the Cheyenne, there was no graver insult to manhood than to dress a buck in woman's clothing. Clearly the others considered him an unmanly coward.

When the rest slept, Matthew could not fight back the hot tears of rage and loneliness and frustration that rolled down his cheeks. He would never be accepted—*never!* If only he had his own weapon he would kill himself and end his intolerable suffering.

By the time the moon was sinking low in the sky, he was numb with exhaustion. His eyes burned from forcing them to stay open. But he knew if he fell asleep, he would not wake in time before Black Elk caught him. And falling asleep on sentry duty meant sure, slow, agonizing death.

Suddenly a shape materialized out of the darkness. Then Little Horse was crouching close by, whispering in his ear.

"Sleep now. I will wake you before Black Elk comes."

Grateful, Matthew tried to thank him. But Little Horse only turned his face away. In no time at all, the weary and thoroughly dejected Matthew fell into a sleep as deep and dreamless as death.

Chapter 11

Soon after Yellow Bear's tribe moved to the Tongue River camp, a Cheyenne word-bringer arrived. He had been sent by Chief Catch the Hawk, whose clan circles were gathered near the Rosebud. Catch the Hawk's people had learned that the surprise Pawnee raid was led by a renegade named War Thunder. War Thunder and his marauding braves had since split up into many smaller bands to avoid detection while waiting to launch their next raid.

The Rosebud River Cheyenne knew these things because their hunters had encountered several isolated groups of Pawnee—all driving stolen Cheyenne ponies before them. They sent in spies who overheard the Pawnee's campfire boasting.

Matthew learned the news during his first brief return to the main camp. Black Elk's band of warriors-in-training had returned to let their ponies graze and rest. Arrow Keeper eyed Matthew's protruding ribs without comment. He and everyone in the camp knew full well what Black Elk and Wolf Who Hunts Smiling were putting the youth through. They had all noticed the glances exchanged by Honey Eater and Matthew—and the murderous jealousy in the eyes of Black Elk when he saw them. And though Wolf Who Hunts Smiling was young, he was strong, and his need to avenge his father's death ran deep into his marrow.

So old Arrow Keeper wisely held his silence. The boy was in a dangerous position and surrounded by enemies. Talk was no good to him. Only manly strength and courage to endure suffering would save him. If he was his father's son, he would survive. If the warrior instincts had been lost to the white man's ways, however, he didn't stand the chance of a sick buffalo set upon by wolves.

Either way, Arrow Keeper was powerless to affect the predetermined outcome of a medicine dream. Only time would tell him if the youth was truly the warrior of his vision at Medicine Lake— or if that were even a true vision. It might have been strong magic placed over his eyes by his enemies.

Unable to bear Matthew's misery, Arrow Keeper did what he could to comfort the youth.

He made sure to keep a fat, juicy buffalo or elk steak constantly sizzling on the tripod outside his tipi entrance while the warriors-in-training remained in camp. The boy divided his brief respite between deep sleeping and ravenous eating in the hopes of restoring himself for the next grueling period of warrior training.

Matthew rallied during the rest in camp.

Thoughts of Bighorn Falls and his former life lost their luster as he renewed his determination to gain acceptance by Yellow Bear's people. But even when his spirits were at their highest, he would spot Wolf Who Hunts Smiling or Black Elk watching him from a distance, and doubt and homesickness would assail him anew.

Soon, however, Matthew earned a measure of revenge against Wolf Who Hunts Smiling—though his victory was brief and left him in greater danger than ever. His triumph came on the first night after Black Elk's band rode out again. Back at the main camp, Black Elk had learned a simple gambling game from a visiting word-bringer, and while Matthew tended the fire and filled the water skins, Black Elk taught it to the others.

He heated two stones in the glowing embers, then rolled them free and let them cool for a few moments. After finding a challenger and arranging a suitable bet, each contestant was to pick up a hot stone and grip it in his fist until one or the other threw it down and lost.

Black Elk first challenged his cousin. It was close, but he won a fine kidskin pouch. From Little Horse, he won a handful of bright beads; from the twins, a cavalry jackknife and a hemp wallet.

Wolf Who Hunts Smiling sulked over the loss of his favorite pouch. To recoup his loss, he bullied the other boys into playing against him. He easily outlasted the twins. But he and Little Horse threw their stones down at the same moment. Despite the draw, Wolf Who Hunts Smiling claimed the bet. He argued hotly that Little Horse had cheated by spitting into his hand first.

Matthew observed the argument as he knelt beside the fire and slid the unburned ends of the logs closer to the blazing middle. He was about to rise and return to his spot beneath a cottonwood ten yards away when Wolf Who Hunts Smiling's mocking voice, speaking in English, froze him in place.

"And what about How-Do-You-Do? Does the brave wounder of ponies wish to challenge a more worthy opponent than his own horse?"

The reminder of his failure with the tomahawk made warm blood creep up the back of his neck. Instead of ignoring his enemy, as usual, Matthew matched his mocking stare and nodded. Little Horse heated the two stones while the bet was arranged. Wolf Who Hunts Smiling offered a new pair of beaded buckskin leggings against the red blanket Arrow Keeper had given Matthew.

After Little Horse rolled the stones free of the embers with a stick, Black Elk nodded, each youth seized a stone and wrapped his fist around it.

The first sensation of blistering heat almost made Matthew drop the stone. But he clenched his jaw and resisted the urge. His lips were pressed straight and tight with determination. Each youth stared into the other's eyes and refused to look away.

The wily, mocking light in Wolf Who Hunts Smiling's eyes transformed itself into surprise when the youth he considered weaker than a woman continued to hold out. Sweat broke out on his brow and gleamed in the dancing firelight.

"Drop it, White Man's Shoes!" Wolf Who Hunts Smiling said, his teeth grinding together in a mixture of pain and determination.

In the past, Matthew would have dropped the stone quickly. But surviving his recent torture by fire had tempered his nerves against the searing pain that night. He recalled the grueling ordeal with Arrow Keeper at Medicine Lake, and the old man's words rang in his head and urged him on: *If you cannot endure this small thing here today, how will you stand and fight when the war cry sounds?* His eyes narrowed to dark, piercing points, and he put the terrible burning sensation outside himself, focusing only on the hatred he felt for his enemy.

With an involuntary cry of pain, Wolf Who Hunts Smiling threw his stone down on the ground. Matthew deliberately waited a full ten heartbeats longer, trembling with pain all the while, before dropping his.

In that brief moment, he enjoyed his first and only triumph since joining Yellow Bear's tribe. Little Horse looked at him with open admiration for the first time. Even the twins were shocked enough to lose their surly stares. They watched the stranger with a new curiosity. Black Elk did not look at him; rather, he aimed a contemptuous glare at his young cousin.

Wolf Who Hunts Smiling rose in fury. He snatched his leggings up off the ground, then turned accusing eyes on Little Horse. As usual, he avoided using names in front of Matthew.

"You! Everyone saw how you deliberately made my stone hotter than the spy's. You are still angry at my earlier victory! The bet is called off!" The next moment, quite deliberately, Wolf Who Hunts Smiling stepped between Matthew and the fire.

Everyone there knew what the gesture meant, and they fell silent at the gravity of the message. Although Wolf Who Hunts Smiling had just announced his intention of killing the intruder, Matthew recalled that Arrow Keeper had said that once he had been warned it was up to him to kill his enemy first.

However, Black Elk had much to teach his band in the next few sleeps, and everyone was too busy to settle any personal scores as they learned the secrets of the buffalo hunt. Black Elk led the youths along an ancient buffalo trail that wound south from the new camp on the Tongue River. They followed the trail and crossed the vast plains between the Bighorn Mountains on the west and the Black Hills on the east.

It was shedding season and thick buffalo fur lay everywhere. It covered the dry riverbeds and rose higher than the ponies' fetlocks. Near the rivers were thick cottonwoods with deep-ridged bark. The herds had backed up against these to scratch and had left them wearing thick fur coats. The huge buffalo wallows were so thick with fur Matthew couldn't see the water.

One morning, they crested a ridge and spotted a vast herd of the bearded monsters running below them. Buffalo always moved in a stampede, Black Elk explained. A few antelopes were running with the herd to seek safety from wolves.

Black Elk opened the ball-and-powder receiver of his side-hammer rifle and loaded it. Then he drew a bead on a straggling cow. Always shoot for the gut, he told the youths. A ball in the rib cage had to hit a vital organ like the heart. But a gut shot bled more and always killed.

And to prove his point, Black Elk dropped the cow with one shot. When the herd had thundered on and the cloud of yellow dust had cleared, the Indians rode down to gather around the carcass. Black Elk taught them the tough job of skinning a buffalo as well as how to stake out the curly hide in order to cure it. Knives and stone chisels were necessary to scrape off every last gobbet of fat or flesh. When it was dry, the skin would be flat and hard, easy to lash to a travois.

The liver was the tenderest and most prized morsel. Black Elk had cut it out first, even before the skinning, and eaten it warm and raw. The other delicacies, including the tongue, the youths cooked and ate immediately. The bulk of the left-over meat would be cut into thin strips and jerked.

Continuing the lesson, Black Elk told of a more ancient way to hunt buffalo that did not require weapons. It was employed when hunters were un-armed, without horses, or could not use their rifles because there was no high ground for cover. Al-though buffalo could not see well, a gunshot would cause them to stampede. If the hunters were on low ground, they stood a good chance of being trampled to death. The solution, Black Elk ex-plained, was to decoy a few buffalo away from the main herd and to run them off a buffalo jump— a blind cliff over which they fell to their death.

One sleep after Black Elk shot the buffalo cow, the Cheyenne youths discovered a perfect cliff only a few hundred yards from the buffalo run, and Black Elk decided to teach his band the ancient decoy tricks used to separate a few animals from the main herd. First it was necessary to find a herd at rest, grazing. Black Elk showed them how to listen for the telltale squawking of buffalo birds that followed the herds and lived off ticks in the buffalo's hide.

Soon they heard the birds on the far side of a long ridge. Making sure to keep his band down-wind of the buffalo, because of the beasts' keen sense of smell, Black Elk led his band to the top of the ridge. Below, in a grassy bottom, a vast herd grazed.

Since they could do nothing until a few animals straggled away from the main herd, they tethered their ponies to graze. Then Black Elk spaced the youths out at careful intervals between the ridge and the blind cliff, placing them at strategic points where the buffalo might veer off and escape. Black Elk sternly warned them to watch for shifts in the wind direction that might give their smell away. Matthew was given the very last spot, a small hill just before the steep drop-off. His job was to run down the hill as the buffalo approached, waving a tree branch to make them veer toward the cliff.

The youth was both excited and determined to perform well. He was still elated from his victory over Wolf Who Hunts Smiling with the hot stones. If he did well in the hunt, the others might change their attitudes toward him.

From his elevated position, Matthew could see everything as it developed. After what seemed like hours, a few buffalo drifted away from the main herd. Black Elk then leaped out from hiding and, shouting and waving his arms, chased the beasts off from the herd.

Matthew watched, his heart pounding with excitement. At a draw where the small herd might have broken across the plains to freedom, Little Horse diverted them back toward the cliff. One by one, Swift Canoe, True Son, and Wolf Who Hunts Smiling leaped from hiding and kept the herd pointed in Matthew's direction.

Dust swirled in high plumes as the animals lumbered closer to him. Concentrating on timing his leap, Matthew was not aware that the wind abruptly shifted directions. He was about to fly down the hill when the buffalo smelled his presence in time to reverse course in a panic. They avoided the cliff and scattered out across the plains.

Stunned, Matthew could only stare, wondering what had gone wrong. Then, he felt the wind pressure on his sweating back and realized his mistake. To make matters worse, the others had all witnessed how his carelessness ruined their hours of patient waiting. As the rest of the band retrieved their horses and rode toward him, Matthew could see the rage in their faces. Even Little Horse gave him an angry stare.

"Woman Face, mighty slayer of ponies!" Black Elk said. His rage-twisted face and the ear sewn with buckskin thread made him look fierce in his wrath. "Did the white men make you such a mighty hunter?"

When Matthew's face flushed hot with shame, Wolf Who Hunts Smiling said, "Look at the woman! She wears her heart in her face!"

Matthew had held his tongue at Black Elk's insults. But since the incident with the hot stones, he had determined to stand up to Wolf Who Hunts Smiling.

"Wolf Who Hunts Smiling barks loud, but lies in his heart like a fox. Everyone saw how he cheated and lied with the stones!"

Wolf Who Hunts Smiling's rage was instant. In a moment, he was off his pony, his knife at the ready. Matthew had learned his fighting style from watching the drunken miners in Bighorn Falls; and he made the mistake of squaring off to box white-man style.

His eyes mocking Matthew, Wolf Who Hunts Smiling casually picked up a rock and threw it at him, hitting his enemy hard in the forehead.

Pain exploded inside Matthew's skull. The day suddenly went blurry, and his legs seemed to lose their bones. The next thing he knew, the ground rushed up to meet him, and he lay there dazed.

Snarling in triumph, Wolf Who Hunts Smiling straddled him and knelt, raising his knife to plunge it.

"No!" Little Horse shouted. He jumped on Wolf Who Hunts Smiling from behind and held on for dear life. But Wolf Who Hunts Smiling was stronger and soon had the smaller boy pinned under him, his knife at the boy's throat.

Black Elk interceded, stopping his cousin's hand from slicing open Little Horse's throat. During their struggles, the blade had opened up a nasty gash on Little Horse's chest.

"He begs for the life of this woman!" protested Wolf Who Hunts Smiling. "He begs for the white man's dog who ruined our hunt!"

Before Black Elk could reply, a hidden rifle spoke its piece, and True Son's white mustang dropped dead where it stood.

Chapter 12

Black Elk, Wolf Who Hunts Smiling, True Son, and Swift Canoe scattered like scalded dogs, scrambling behind hummocks and isolated cottonwoods. With the aid of Little Horse, Matthew made it to cover, even though he was still stunned from his injury. The shot had come from high up in the rimrock behind them. The youths craned their necks and squinted up into the bright sunlight, expecting a hail of lead.

Instead, they saw two Pawnee braves, stripped to their breechclouts, standing atop a huge pile of rock debris at the bottom of a sheer cliff. Sunlight glinted off a whiskey bottle as one passed it to the other. They were taking turns firing their rifles, apparently just to make noise. They acted as if they had not spotted the Cheyenne even though they had just shot True Son's horse.

Another shot split the silence, and a bullet flew

past the Cheyenne with a sound like an angry hornet. Only then did they realize that a ricochet had dropped the pony. Soon the two Pawnee mounted their spotted horses and headed up into the high country, disappearing behind another pile of debris.

Black Elk gathered his band for a hurried council, the near-fatal confrontation between Matthew, Wolf Who Hunts Smiling, and Little Horse long forgotten. Black Elk's face showed fierce determination to gain revenge against their hereditary enemy.

It was important, Black Elk explained, to track the Pawnee back to their trail camp. Their strength and numbers would have to be learned and reported to the headmen back at Yellow Bear's camp. Despite the bloodlust gleaming in his dark eyes, Black Elk was a true Cheyenne warrior. The idea of striking without painting and dressing for battle and making an offering to the Medicine Arrows frightened him. He did not fear death, but the prospect of dying without strong medicine. For the warrior who did so had to wander forever by himself in the Forest of Tears. To be kept out of the Land of Ghosts was worse than being banished from an earthly tribe. True death for an Indian was to be alone forever. Still, they had to locate the camp of the Pawnee raiders.

"We are not white-livered cowards. We are Cheyenne!" Black Elk told his band.

He stared at Matthew, perhaps recalling how his enemy had recently stood up to Wolf Who Hunts Smiling. "It is not enough to talk the he-bear talk. A warrior's skill is in the doing, not the talking."

Since True Son's pony had been killed, Black

Elk ordered him to share mounts with the other four youths until they could replace his pony. Then, single file and well apart, the youths followed Black Elk toward the point where they had seen the two Pawnee up in the rimrock.

From a distance, Matthew could detect no possible way of scaling the sheer rock face on horseback. But when the band drew nearer, they discovered a narrow, hidden trail. It wound and twisted way up the rimrock in a series of steep switchbacks. As they climbed higher and higher, Matthew felt cool sweat break out in his armpits. At any moment, he expected a rifle ball to shatter his skull.

No one talked so as to remain constantly vigilant and aware of his surroundings. They listened carefully to every noise, studied every movement, even occasionally paused so Black Elk could sniff the air. It was said he could actually smell Pawnee warrior, when the wind was right.

Matthew marveled at Black Elk's ability to read signs. There were no obvious clues, such as fresh horse droppings, to tell how recent each set of tracks was. But Black Elk could tell how old each print was by judging how far the mud had settled in any track. Twice he motioned to the others to stop while he climbed up high in the sloping debris to get a better view before riding on.

No skill was required to spot the many empty whiskey bottles littering the trail. Matthew hoped it was careless drunkenness that gave the Pawnee away, not a clever plan to lure the Cheyenne to their deaths.

After the trail finally leveled off and wound through a narrow defile, the band traversed another series of cliffs crowded with limestone outcroppings. Soon they were climbing again. The trail narrowed until it wasn't even safe for sure-footed mules.

When they were so high up that wind-twisted trees grew from cracks in the rocks, they encountered an old antelope buck that blocked their trial. It failed to run away as they approached. Instead, the animal constantly stared at something on the ground as it circled around and around.

"Snake," said Black Elk without bothering to investigate.

The band detoured carefully around the reptile swinging wide so their ponies wouldn't nicker and give them away. But, for all their precautions, Matthew knew they might well be already in the sights of Pawnee lookouts.

The sun sank low as they progressed. When it was out of sight behind the rock-tipped cones of the Bighorns, the young Cheyenne discovered a clearing where a good-sized camp had been made. But there was no danger, Black Elk concluded after a quick examination. He pointed out several fresh animal tracks that wouldn't be present in such numbers if men had been there recently.

As the band journied onward, they arrived at a point where the crude trail jutted out close to the edge of the rock face again. There, Matthew could see everything that lay below, and for the first time in his life, he realized how truly beautiful and majestic the land was. The Tongue River Valley wound like a green ribbon across the broad dull-brown expanse of the endless plains. Captivated, Matthew began to feel as if he could soar out over the land like the hawks and eagles. But at the same time, he also felt his own insignificance. In the grand scheme of the universe, he meant no more

115

than a bug inching its way up a cliff until it was crushed beneath another animal's foot.

In the first grainy twilight of early evening, Black Elk suddenly lifted one hand to halt the youths. Without a word he pointed dead ahead toward a huge circle of scrub oaks where the trail appeared to end. Using hand signals, he had the band back up about 50 yards down the trail. The others followed him as he left the trail and found a small but lush patch of gama grass. There, they hobbled their tired ponies with strips of rawhide and let them graze.

Again warning his charges to remain completely silent, Black Elk led them on foot back to the copse of oaks. They slipped in amongst the trees and peered out toward a grassy clearing on the other side. The high-altitude camp was in a perfect defensive position. Any attack from the south was impossible without scaling the other side of the mountain. The east and west approaches were equally inaccessible because of cliffs and jagged heaps of rock debris. Any attack would have to be mounted up the narrow trail on the northern slope.

At least 20 Pawnee braves milled about the grassy clearing. Behind them stood wickiups that consisted of tree-branch frames covered with grass and brush. That style of construction was common among the tribes of the Southwest like the Southern Pawnee who had raided Yellow Bear's camp. But what convinced Black Elk and the others that they had found the camp of their enemies was the dozen or so ponies in a temporary rope corral. Without doubt, they were the buckskins and duns and white mustangs stolen from the Cheyenne.

Although it was nearly dark, Matthew could see

the Pawnee's greased top-knots shine when they passed close to the firelight. In the center of camp, the Pawnee had dug several holes, thrown a deer's head in each, and raked coals over them. After cooking the deer heads, they devoured the tongues, eyes, and roasted brains and washed the victuals down with the white man's devil water, which made several of them act crazy drunk.

One of the Pawnee was older and fiercer looking than the others. He was a scarred but vigorous warrior in his middle years. Unlike the others, who wore only breechclouts and moccasins, he also wore an elaborate cape made of scalps. The Cheyenne hiding in the trees knew the scalps with the freshest blood were those of their Powder River kinsmen.

The word-bringer had mentioned that War Thunder wore such a cape of human trophies to unnerve his enemies in battle. With a cool shudder of fear and hatred, Matthew recalled the carnage visited upon his people and Honey Eater's heart-rending grief for her dead mother and the others. He would gladly take the scalp of the man who had caused such devastation.

Black Elk too had spied the renegade leader and realized his luck. Before them was the band of Pawnee warriors who had spilled great amounts of Cheyenne blood. Surely, the warrior who exacted revenge for the tribe would be honored all of his days. And since their enemies were crazy from paleface strong water, Black Elk and his band could not fail in their attempt to strike back. At the same time, he would also teach his young bucks the most important lesson in Cheyenne warfare.

Moving silently, he touched all of them and signaled them to follow him. They dropped back to a small moonlit clearing where Black Elk could speak in low tones. Behind them, the Pawnee camp grew louder as whiskey flowed freely.

"Young brothers, hear me well!"

The words secretly impressed Matthew. It was a rare mark of respect for a blooded warrior to address his subordinates as brothers. And for the first time, Matthew had felt included in such an important council.

"You know that treading the warpath at night can anger the Great Spirit and turn a Cheyenne *wendigo*—make him crazy for life. And day or night, Cheyenne never attack without painting and dressing and praying to the Medicine Arrows.

"But young brothers, there is something even braver than the kill, something even better than the kill. There is something which says to your enemy, 'I have mastered you, I have humiliated you, and only when I choose will I also kill you!'"

Black Elk explained that the highest honor in battle was to count coup on an enemy, which could be done in several ways. A warrior could strike his enemy a symbolic blow with quirt, bow, or knife before being attacked; a warrior could strip his enemy of all his weapons or steal his horse. But the gravest, most devastating insult of all was to steal an enemy's medicine bag while he slept, thus destroying his magic protection forever.

After a warrior had successfully counted coup, he achieved the right to wear an eagle feather in his hair. Every time he counted coup thereafter, he received another feather. But it was a disgrace to fail at counting coup. Many warriors preferred to die, Black Elk informed the youths solemnly.

For such a failure was the warrior's mark of shame.

That night, he added, would be their first true test as warriors. He, Wolf Who Hunts Smiling, Little Horse, Swift Canoe, and Matthew would wait until the camp was asleep. Then each was to slip in and steal a brave's medicine bag or weapons. True Son, in the meantime, would count coup by stealing a pony to replace his dead one. Black Elk cautioned them twice against killing that night, his eyes finding Wolf Who Hunt's Smiling's in the moonlight. That would come in good time.

Matthew's pulse thudded loudly in his ears as they resumed their former positions at the edge of camp. A faint, rhythmic sound to his right made him strain to see in the dim ruby glow of the camp fires. Then he realized that Wolf Who Hunts Smiling was honing his knife on the fine-grained stone he always carried in his legging sash. After Black Elk's strict order to avoid killing, Wolf Who Hunts Smiling's actions troubled Matthew and reminded him that he had no weapons for his own defense.

Despite their increasing drunkenness, the Pawnee braves below were careful to keep a weapon always at hand. It was their first consideration even as they relaxed or fell asleep. Their marauding life-style forced them to always keep their backs to a tree or rock, thus covering all approaches to them.

Fortunately for the Cheyenne, the high, isolated camp had lulled the Pawnee into a sense of security, and they posted no sentries. The moon had crawled much farther up in the sky before the camp fell silent. Finally Black Elk made the soft, clicking sound of a tree lizard—the signal to advance.

As he followed Black Elk toward the dying glow of the fires, Matthew reached to feel his own medicine bag for courage. Then, like the others, he dropped down on all fours and crept closer. Blood throbbed in his ears, and his calves felt like water.

Wolf Who Hunts Smiling was a dark form on his right, Little Horse a smaller shape on his left. They advanced silently, the night grass cool and damp against their bare skin. Sweat poured out of Matthew's raggedly cropped hair and trickled into his eyes, burning them.

The fires were almost dead, making it difficult to distinguish shapes. Matthew moved toward the nearest stream of loud snoring. Every nerve ending in his body was raw with expectation.

When his groping hand struck warm buffalo fur, a Pawnee muttered in his sleep. Matthew froze and his heart scampered like a frenzied rat. Finally the ragged snoring resumed.

Sweat beading into his eyes, he waited for the wind to blow several clouds away from in front of the moon. Slowly, as silver moonlight washed over the camp, he realized that the Pawnee had passed out in a drunken stupor, half out of his robes. His medicine bag was visible. Matthew relaxed slightly—liquor had made his task easier.

At that moment, he glanced to his right and almost cried out. Wolf Who Hunts Smiling was eerily clear in the ghostly light. He had risen to a crouch over his sleeping victim and unsheathed his knife. Matthew realized he meant to kill the Pawnee and raise his scalp!

Wolf Who Hunts Smiling was convinced he could kill quickly and silently and obtain an important trophy for his clan's lodge pole. Despite Black Elk's strict command, he knew his cousin would be proud of him afterward. He would simply lie and say his victim woke up, forcing him to kill in his own defense.

He didn't count on the Pawnee's cunning. For the Pawnee had circled his robes with dried seed pods. As Wolf Who Hunts Smiling approached the drunken Indian, he crushed one of the pods with his heel.

Awakened by the crackling, the Pawnee instantly raised a hideous warning shriek. All around the camp other braves leaped up and kicked glowing embers into flames. Matthew saw Little Horse, a captured lance and bow in his hands, break for the oak trees. Black Elk was right behind him, clutching a brave's muzzle-loader.

True Son was clearing the corral leading a buckskin pony. He mounted the pony and dug his heels into its flanks. But before he could escape a rifle spat fire, and True Son snapped backwards to the ground, arms flung wide. His heels scratched the ground for a few moments before he died.

Wolf Who Hunts Smiling barely managed to jump back in time when the brave he had awoken grabbed for his ankle. As more rifles spoke into the night, Wolf Who Hunts Smiling bolted for the trees, Matthew right behind him. One image burned itself into both boys' minds when the Pawnee warrior rose in the moonlight to chase them: the cape their enemy wore was covered with scalps.

Chapter 13

Luck was with Black Elk's band. The Pawnee marauders, experts at deception themselves, suspected the nighttime raid was merely a decoy to lure them into an ambush. So they refused to give chase beyond their protective circle of scrub oak.

The Cheyenne were able to retrieve their horses and escape without further bloodshed. They made the long, moonlit trek back down the steep trail. Then they raced north to bring word of War Thunder and his band to the main camp. Unfortunately for Matthew, however, new troubles began at dawn when Black Elk halted his band to water their ponies in the Little Bighorn River.

"Woman Face caused the death of True Son!" Wolf Who Hunts Smiling said to his cousin and the others. "I saw everything! As I was about to untie my enemy's medicine bag, I saw him shake his brave's shoulder until he woke him up. This proves Woman Face is a spy and hopes to seize the opportunity to have us killed. Only then can he escape."

"Then may the white man's spy die of the yellow vomit!" Swift Canoe said, anger smoldering in his eyes. "His deception has killed my brother!"

Black Elk seized the youth when he leaped at Matthew. "Enough! Will you wail like an old squaw when your brother died like a warrior? Stop this unmanly display of feelings close to your heart. Our first duty now is to report our enemies to the headmen."

He cast a cold-eyed glance at Matthew. "We will discuss these other matters in council also."

Matthew was too angry at Wolf Who Hunts Smiling to bother defending himself. Not only was Wolf Who Hunts Smiling lying, but he had no doubt enraged War Thunder so much that the Pawnee leader would once again attack Yellow Bear's people. Matthew was sure Wolf Who Hunts Smiling had seen that cape of human scalps. But who would believe him, Woman Face?

The youths arrived back at their camp by midmorning. Immediately the camp crier notified Yellow Bear and Arrow Keeper of their arrival, then rode up and down the clan circles announcing an emergency council. Arrow Keeper, Yellow Bear, the clan headmen assembled, and the adult braves met in their new council lodge. The gathering was considerably smaller than the one before the Powder River massacre. But Black Elk's band, as warriors in training, were permitted to attend to answer the subchiefs' questions.

Matthew was coldly ignored by everyone in the lodge, for Wolf Who Hunts Smiling had spread his lie. Unable to stand the scorn, Matthew returned

123

to the tipi he shared with Arrow Keeper. Although no one had yet formally accused him of any crime, he knew the men would discuss him at the council, and no doubt they would decide his fate once again with the stones.

As usual, women and children were not permitted at the council. Nonetheless, at a back corner of the council lodge where two elk skins did not quite overlap on their branch frame, Honey Eater crouched, breathlessly listening for every word from within.

Her jet-black hair was braided with white columbine, and shells and colored stones adorned her dress. Her pretty face went tense with panic when a stray cloud of smoke from inside wafted into her nostrils and almost made her cough. It was the rich, strong smell of white man's tobacco. She liked the scent, but it always took her by surprise.

She knew that the tall stranger would be discussed that day. She had heard the charges against him passed on from tipi to tipi like fire leaping through dry grass. He was accused not only of causing True Son's death, but of forcing Black Elk's band to disgrace the entire tribe as well. No Cheyenne ever left their dead alone anywhere, much less among enemies who would surely mutilate the body. True Son would never enter the Land of Ghosts, but must roam alone with his soul in pain forever.

Honey Eater shuddered at the enormity of True Son's horrible fate. Such a charge against the newcomer would not be treated lightly. Besides that, had she not seen the angry, swollen lump on his forehead and the ragged gash on Little Horse's chest? Whatever the problem, the fiery hatred in the eyes of Wolf Who Hunts Smiling told her there would be trouble for the handsome newcomer.

So, ignoring the risk, she dared to eavesdrop on the council. If she were caught, her place as the chief's daughter would not save her from punishment; rather, it would make the tribe's wrath greater. She thought of Eagle in Flight of the Deer Clan. He had cut off his squaw's nose for lying with another brave. The punishment for her sin would be even greater. But as the council progressed, her fears for Matthew seemed wasted, for the talk within was all of war.

"These Pawnee must be hunted out like wild dogs!" a clan leader declared. "It is not only their attack on our former camp that we must avenge. They have been stealing from our traps in the beaver ponds. Like the blue-eyes, they slaughter one buffalo for a few morsels of meat. Soon they will leave us chewing the strings from our own buckskins for nourishment."

His argument was met with shouts of strong agreement.

"We must strike War Thunder now while his numbers are small!" Honey Eater heard another say. "Our enemies blackened their faces against us first. Now let us grease their bones with war paint."

More shouts of approval rang out. Soon, with her father's calm voice occasionally imposing order, plans for war were made. A war chief would be named by Yellow Bear, who had been chosen as a peace leader only. The important Medicine Arrows ceremony would be conducted by Arrow Keeper that night. Early the next day, the braves would prepare for battle and ride out.

The battle plans decided, the men considered other matters. Honey Eater tensed when she recognized the voice of Swift Canoe. She was sorry his brother had died an unclean death. But she had never liked or trusted either of the twins. Their Wolverine Clan were known among the village as complainers who always shirked hard work and loved to stir up trouble.

"Fathers! Please hear my plea. The death of my brother, True Son, must be avenged. Fathers! Hear the words Wolf Who Hunts Smiling has for you. They are true words which you may put in your sashes and carry away with you."

Honey Eater listened, her face a mask of concern, as Wolf Who Hunts Smiling repeated his account of Matthew's supposed treachery. When he fell silent, a long and angry murmur filled the lodge, and from amid the rumble of voices, Little Horse spoke out calmly.

"Fathers! Hear me well. It is true Little Horse could not see everything which happened in the Pawnee camp. But he knows that Wolf Who Hunts Smiling likes to speak with more than one tongue. The one Arrow Keeper has named Touch the Sky makes many mistakes, but he is one of us. His heart is strong and true, and he speaks one way always."

"You say these things because I put the wound on your chest," retorted Wolf Who Hunts Smiling. "I say he is a spy and we should kill him!"

Old Arrow Keeper had deliberately held his silence until that moment. He had decided to trust in the power of his medicine dream. Either it was a true dream, or it was strong magic placed over his eyes. Like Yellow Bear, he knew the young men must have their say. But now, the medicine man addressed himself to Black Elk.

"Your young cousin has the hot temper of your

clan, certainly. But the bitter things he has seen
have bent him, as a rough wind bends a tender
shoot. Now there is nothing but hard bark on
him."

"Hard bark, father," Black Elk answered
proudly, "can repel an arrow."

Honey Eater decided to listen to no more. She
had heard enough to fear the outcome. Dark
clouds were gathering. She had to act before the
storm broke. She slipped away from the council
lodge and left to warn Matthew.

Matthew remained inside the sweat lodge until
the last wisps of steam were gone and the red-hot
rocks had grown cold. He was soaked from scalp
to soles. It was almost as if he had tried to sweat
the white man's influence out of himself, leaving
nothing but Cheyenne behind. But fear and doubts
plagued him as he emerged from the sweat lodge
and wiped himself down with sagebrush.

Naked, he headed toward the river to plunge in
for a cooling rinse. He knew full well the rest of
the camp was either attending the council or ea-
gerly awaiting its decisions. He also knew the men
were discussing him at the council. The only rea-
son they had not tied him up again was their respect for Arrow Keeper.

But how long, Matthew wondered, would the
old medicine man remain his friend—especially
since the rest of the tribe resented Arrow Keeper
for protecting a suspected spy. The lies Wolf Who
Hunts Smiling was no doubt telling about him
would only make matters worse.

Matthew paused where the grassy bank gave
way to the streaming river. The water moved
quickly, it was cool and clean, but still tinted

brown from the spring soil runoff. The opposite bank was a wall of dense thickets that appeared inpenetrable. But in fact, behind it lay secret escape trails. Every Cheyenne in camp old enough to walk knew of their location.

Again Matthew recalled Arrow Keeper's teachings. He tried to free his mind of thoughts and pay attention instead to the language of nature. He could pick out the harsh calls of willets and grebes and hawks, the soft warblings of orioles and thrushes and purple finches. But even as he slipped, sweaty and hot, into the cold water, his mind returned to one problem like a tongue to a chipped tooth. Was he a white man or a Cheyenne? Or was he neither, an outcast rejected by both races?

When the water reached the middle of his thighs, he ducked the rest of his body under for a long time, letting the swift current cleanse his sweaty pores. He stood up again, and the breeze blew cool against his wet skin. He shook his head once to clear his eyes of water.

Abruptly, a flock of sandpipers rose in a nervous jerk from the grassy bank behind him. Matthew whirled around. Then he froze as still as a startled deer when he saw a figure watching him.

Recognizing Honey Eater, he instinctively squatted down to hide his nakedness. Though her eyes were cast modestly downward, she made no effort to flee. She called something to him, but her words were lost in the rushing current. A moment later, she surprised him even more by wading out toward him.

For a moment, he forgot his training and let disbelief show in his face. He watched her draw nearer, her pretty, finely sculpted face urgent with

some message for him. He watched the water soak
her buckskin dress and make it cling like a second
skin to her slender thighs. When she stood close
enough to touch him, he could smell the fragrant
white columbine petals in her hair.

"You must go," she said. "Go while you can.
Leave this place forever!"

It was the first time he had heard her speak. Her
voice was gentle like a breeze through tall grass,
but her message disturbed him.

"Why must I leave?"

"The council goes badly. Some speak for you,
but they are not many. If the stones are allowed
to speak, it will mean trouble for you. You must
run now!"

Still crouching awkwardly, he stared at the
maiden until she finally met his eyes. "Why do
you come here? If you are caught it means trouble
for you also."

The question made blood rush to her face, but
she ignored it. "It is Wolf Who Hunts Smiling. He
has spoken against you. He says you are a spy,
that you killed True Son with your treachery."

For a long moment, Matthew was silent as he
recalled the night when Wolf Who Hunts Smiling
had stepped between him and the fire. The hotheaded young Cheyenne was determined to kill
him. "Do you believe these things he says about
me?"

Honey Eater met his eyes for a moment before
she looked away and shook her head. "No. It is
true that I do not know you. But I feel in my heart
that you are not capable of these things he says.
But the others do not feel as I do. You must leave
this place at once!"

Their eyes met again, and this time she did not

look away so quickly. Matthew watched a vein pulse in the soft smooth skin of her throat. The current was swift and Honey Eater moved slightly the wrong way, stepping on a slippery rock that threw her off balance.

She stumbled and was about to fall, but Matthew reached out, easily catching her. She felt light as a reed. While she was in his grasp, the current moved them together, and he felt the firm curves of her body against his naked flesh.

"I must return," she said, stepping back out of his arms. "Please promise that you will flee at once."

He could not speak. The burning touch of her flesh had left his throat tight with sudden desire. But when his blood finally cooled, he felt nothing but determination. He had been forced to leave the only family he knew and the girl he loved; he had suffered torture and humiliation and unjust accusations; everywhere his enemies were plotting against him.

Then let them plot, Matthew decided. All the unjust treatment had left him bitter and hardened. He was sick of running. He would fight his enemies and win—no matter how much he had to sacrifice to do so.

Honey Eater read his thoughts in his eyes. Before she turned around to wade back to shore, she pleaded one more time. "You must flee. I fear the stones will demand your death."

With that she hurried away as fast as the current would permit. But Matthew shouted above the bubbling chuckle of the river, "Never! I will run away no more. I will die first!"

Chapter 14

Before the stones could speak against Matthew, a youth from the Lightning Bolt Clan boldly lifted the elk-skin flap away from the entrance of the council lodge. His eyes were wide with urgency.

"Fathers! Come at once. Red Pony is back with a message. Come quickly! He is dying."

The headmen's surprise at being interrupted in council gave way to swift action. Yellow Bear and the councillors hurried outside to the middle of camp, where Red Pony lay with his head on a rolled-up blanket. An ugly swelling high on his chest marked the spot a lead ball had struck.

Within moments, almost everyone in camp had crowded around the new arrival. Honey Eater had just returned from the river when she heard the commotion, and Matthew also hurried up from the river to see what was happening.

He recognized Red Pony at once. The young

brave was in charge of the hunting party that went out early each morning. The hunters returned near dark, sometimes after, with their catch lashed to a travois. It was clear he had lost much blood and would die despite the efforts of the old squaw tending to him.

"Yellow Bear!" he said when he recognized the chief. "Our enemies surround us. No one may enter or leave our camp. The others were killed. But I was able to hide and then crawl back before their guards were in place."

Despite his age, Yellow Bear easily dropped into a squat beside the dying brave. Red Pony's hard journey back had left his voice weak.

"Which enemies, little brother?" the chief said.

"Pawnee, Father! I could hear their talk while they searched for me. War Thunder is like a sore-tailed bear in his anger. The lice-eaters say their leader woke to find a brazen Cheyenne buck preparing to raise his scalp. Now War Thunder must have his revenge."

Upon hearing Red Pony's words, Black Elk stared at his young cousin. Had Wolf Who Hunts Smiling defied his order not to kill during the raid on the Pawnee camp? If Black Elk expected an answer, he was disappointed, for Wolf Who Hunts Smiling remained as impassive as a carved totem, his face revealing nothing.

"Our camp is surrounded?" Yellow Bear said. "You are sure of this? Where are the sentries?"

"Dead or captured, Father. War Thunder waits only for the other scattered bands to join him. They are expected in perhaps two sleeps. His band is enough to ring us and stop us from fleeing until the rest arrive. They have even found where our escape trails end. This time, War Thunder swears, the scalp of Yellow Bear will adorn his cape!"

The cracked-leather worry lines in Yellow Bear's face deepening, he addressed Arrow Keeper.

"War Thunder is clever like a fox. We do not have the braves to fight him. He knows well that even if we could send a messenger through his guards, no one could help us. Catch the Hawk's Cheyenne, on the Rosebud, and Spring Dance's Lakota have combined for a huge hunt north of the Yellowstone. Both have sent word they will not return until the Moon of the Red Cherries."

Yellow Bear, Arrow Keeper, and several senior headmen spoke quietly but urgently among themselves. While the elders conferred, Matthew spotted a small but sturdy form and worked his way through the others until he stood beside Little Horse. Wolf Who Hunts Smiling immediately noticed them. He nudged Swift Canoe with his elbow, and they approached the other two.

"Why not pet the white man's dog?" Wolf Who Hunts Smiling said to Little Horse. His furtive eyes flashed constantly back and forth between them. "At the council you spoke up for him against your own Cheyenne brother."

Swift Canoe stared coldly at Matthew. Clearly he was not worried about the tribe's dilemma. Instead, he was angry that the new emergency had arrived before his enemy could be condemned for the death of his brother.

Before Little Horse could reply to Wolf Who Hunts Smiling's taunt, Yellow Bear's voice silenced all talk. "Brothers! Hear the words I tell you. Then pick them up and hold them close to your breast. A medicine dream has told me I will not live to see the next greening of the grass. Perhaps my death is now at hand. But while I have light in my eyes, I serve my people.

"Warriors! Make ready your battle rigs. Now Yellow Bear's people will turn to their new war chief."

He crossed to where Black Elk stood surrounded by his followers. "Black Elk is younger than I was when I first counted coup against the Crow at Crazy Woman Fork. But he is the fiercest, bravest warrior among us. Now he will lead his people in this terrible trial."

Black Elk's eyes were fierce with proud triumph. "Brothers!" he said. "Hear me well. We have lost many, and the fight will be hard. We are trapped here, surrounded. We will fight, and when we fall it will be on our enemies. Their blood will flow with ours, and so long as one Cheyenne buck breathes, the fight will not be over."

His words were brave, and the few warriors still left raised a shout of approval. But Matthew watched Yellow Bear and Arrow Keeper exchange long, deeply troubled looks. Black Elk's he-bear talk did not fool them, he realized. Only a miracle could save the tribe from doom.

Black Elk issued instructions for fortifying the camp and making ready for the war dance. Normally a Cheyenne buck would have at least 16 winters behind him before he was required to do battle. But that night, all the males over 12 would join the blooded warriors in praying to the arrows.

In the battle to come, there could be no such thing as a running battle, Black Elk warned the men. The escape routes were cut off, there was no place to run. It would be a fight to the death.

Matthew's blood chilled when two old Cheyenne squaws began keening in grief. More sadness so soon after the bloody Powder River massacre was too cruel for them to bear. They mourned not for their own tired old bones, but for the children and the young people who were the future of the tribe.

Troubled, Matthew watched Little Horse and the others hurry to make ready their equipment. He wanted to ask Arrow Keeper about a weapon he too could use in battle. But the medicine man was busy conferring with Yellow Bear and the headmen.

Matthew walked down to the river and sat in silence for a long time, listening to the laughing current and thinking many worrisome thoughts. But one thought loomed larger than all the others: Yellow Bear's people, Matthew included, would soon be food for buzzards unless a miracle could be worked.

When the plan came to Matthew, it came all at once. He didn't waste time debating it. His mouth set straight and tight with determination, Matthew slipped back to the tipi he shared with Arrow Keeper. The medicine man still had not returned. The youth rummaged under Arrow Keeper's buffalo robes until he found the bone-handle knife the old man had used to pick the buckshot out of Matthew's back. Placing the knife in his legging sash along with pemmican and dried plums, he slipped back down to the river.

He didn't bother stopping at the pony corral. It would be difficult enough to escape the Pawnee circle on foot, much less on horseback. His plan was to evade the Pawnee, then work his way downriver south toward the Sioux village at Elbow Bend. There he would obtain a horse and make his way to Bighorn Falls.

The thought of returning to his home made a tight lump fill his throat. But he knew his plan was the only chance the tribe had of surviving. If he could make it in time—and if he could avoid the hidden enemy all around him—Yellow Bear's people might not be destroyed.

Matthew reached the fast-streaming water and cautiously scanned the opposite bank for spies before he stepped out into the open. A few moments of searching turned up a good-sized log. He dragged it out from its matted cover of leaves, then rolled it into the water and slipped in behind it. His plan was to hang on and stay hidden in the water. But as he was about to launch the log out into the middle of the current, a voice called out from shore and stopped him.

"Wolf Who Hunts Smiling spoke the straight word," Little Horse said, his old muzzle-loader pointed at Matthew. "You are a spy—or a white-livered coward who runs to save himself while his people die."

"I am no spy," Matthew said, "and I am not running away. I have a plan to save Yellow Bear's people."

"What is this plan?" Little Horse said coldly, clearly not believing him.

"There is no time now to explain. I must leave before it is too late."

"Lies! And I spoke for you in front of the headmen and warriors. I said you were one of us, that your heart was strong and true. Never will they believe me again."

Anger warmed his blood, but Matthew held his face expressionless in the Indian fashion. He started to push the log out again. Little Horse raised his rifle menacingly.

"Stop!" he said. "I will kill you before I let you go."

Matthew watched his Cheyenne brother for a long moment. Despite his youth and small size, Little Horse was impressive in his compact strength and the determined set of his face.

"Perhaps you will shoot me," Matthew said finally. "But if you do, you will surely kill our tribe's only chance for survival."

The words were spoken sincerely and had a clear impact on Little Horse. Doubt flickered in his intense dark eyes even as he aimed his rifle.

"Look at me!" Matthew said. "Have you ever known me as a liar? Have I ever played the coward?"

Little Horse was a long time answering. His sense of fair play was starting to win out over anger.

"You have made mistakes, surely," he finally said, "as an untaught child will. But you have always spoken one way and never shown the white feather."

"Then, will you let me go if I give my word to return now?"

Little Horse debated awhile before saying, "Your scalp will end up on a Pawnee coup stick."

"Perhaps. But it surely will if I do nothing."

"You speak the truth," Little Horse said, and then he surprised Matthew by adding, "but if you are a spy, I cannot let you out of my sight. If you speak straight arrow, I cannot stop you. Therefore, I am going with you."

Little Horse slung his rifle high on his back. Then he waded into the river. "Now quickly, speak of this plan."

By the time the sun was casting long shadows, Yellow Bear's Cheyenne were all working with a grim sense of purpose. Careful probing by scouts had verified Red Pony's story. They were indeed surrounded.

The women gathered to make bullets in the lodge where they usually sewed and made jewelry. Boys not old enough to pray to the arrows dug rifle pits beyond the first circle of tipis. Behind the pits, facing the only line of attack from the north, they erected log breastworks.

That night, the clay pipes would stay lit all night. So two old squaws sat in front of a tipi mixing tobacco with dried bark. By nightfall a huge fire blazed in the middle of the camp. The blooded warriors showed up carrying their decorated shields and wearing their crow-feather bonnets, which would have to be blessed with the correct medicine.

Arrow Keeper solemnly watched the warriors and young bucks assemble. His heart was sad and troubled. Except briefly, earlier in the day, he had not seen Matthew. But the youth's absence was the least of his worries. Hurrying the Medicine Arrow ceremony was wrong. War was serious business, and Arrow Keeper wished he could first have spoken with the water spirits at Medicine Lake.

He wore a special calico shirt painted with magic symbols. His face was greased as the warriors' would be against the attack—his forehead yellow, his nose red, his chin black. His single-horned headdress contained 40 feathers in its tail.

Honey Eater and a young girl from the Crooked Lance Clan served as maids of honor at the ceremony. It was their job to keep time with stone-filled gourds while the warriors danced with their knees kicking high. Beaded buckskins glinted in the firelight as the men chanted their war cry over and over in a rhythm that soon lulled the observers into a trance.

During the ceremony, Arrow Keeper would make his most powerful medicine so the Pawnee bullets could not find his people. From that night until the attack, the braves would fast. Hunger would make them weak and lightheaded, but it would also purify them and give them the ability to endure battle better.

Despite his great concern for the tribe, Matthew's absence nagged at him. Had the dream at Medicine Lake been a false omen. Had the youth he believed to be a great warrior turned out to be a coward after all? If that was true, the tribe was doomed. They were low on warriors, rifles, and ammunition. They would never survive a battle against the well-armed and numerous Pawnee.

His heart as heavy as a stone, Arrow Keeper unwrapped the coyote-fur pouch that contained the four sacred Medicine Arrows. He lay them on a stump near the fire. One by one, all the males of 12 winters or more, except the white-haired elders, lined up behind the arrows. Arrow Keeper prayed out loud in a singsong chant to the Great Spirit, beseeching courage for the upcoming battle. Then each male took turns filing by and making an offering to the arrows.

The men and boys knelt to leave bright beads, twists of rich tobacco, a twelve-feathered eagle tail, a tanned buffalo robe, a pair of leggings, a blanket, a knife, a dressed deerskin, a beaver pelt. When all of them had filed by, Black Elk spoke up above the rhythm of the gourds. "Where are Woman Face and Little Horse?"

Swift Canoe and Wolf Who Hunts Smiling were sent to scour the camp. They returned without the missing youths. "Like rabbits they run away from danger!" Wolf Who Hunts Smiling cried.

Black Elk, who had hardly taken his eyes off Honey Eater since she arrived, watched her with a triumphant gleam in his eyes. For her part, she could barely restrain hot, bitter tears of disappointment at Matthew's apparent desertion. He had run away and left the tribe to die!

"It is better this way," said Black Elk so all could hear his mocking tone. "The great warrior would only end up killing his own pony!"

The other warriors murmured their agreement and scorn, but old Arrow Keeper wisely kept silent, his painted and weather-lined face as impassive as a leather mask.

Chapter 15

While Yellow Bear's Cheyenne prepared for battle, Matthew and Little Horse were desperately fighting to avoid death along the river. Since War Thunder knew that any escape attempt would probably be by water, Pawnee sentries had been stationed at intervals along the Tongue. The two Cheyenne slipped past the first without incident, clinging to the far side of their log and staying low in the water.

But trouble threatened the youths when they reached the second sentry. The Pawnee was waiting at a bend in the river where a large tree stood caught in the river, its branches sawing back and forth with the water. The outspread branches of the sawyer had trapped a swirling mass of debris, and the youths' log was heading straight for it. Spotting the imminent danger in the nick of time, they began kicking their legs mightily underwater,

141

straining their lean upper bodies to force the log around.

For a moment, they were snared by the debris, and all forward motion stopped. Matthew and Little Horse heaved, and with a slow, rolling movement sideways, the log eased around the sawyer and past the sentry.

The victory left both boys elated. But the effort also reminded Matthew that he was dangerously near exhaustion. The night before had been spent raiding the Pawnee camp, and he had not slept one wink since. As a result, his head felt light, just as it had during the day-long ordeal in the sun at Medicine Lake. But thinking of Medicine Lake also reminded him that Arrow Keeper had made him endure that pain to prove that he could. Having succeeded once in the face of terrible adversity he was determined to succeed again.

Matthew was all the more willing to risk his life because Little Horse was helping him. Little Horse had listened to his daring plan in silence, offering no words of approval. Although he appeared to believe they stood little chance, he had not turned back. As desperate as the plan seemed, Little Horse must have realized it was the tribe's only chance, and he would do anything to save his people. But even that slim hope appeared doomed when they spotted another sentry.

Armed with a U.S. Cavalry carbine, the Pawnee waited at the brisk rapids just before the juncture at Beaver Creek. The juncture was an excellent defensive position because the huge underwater boulders would block canoes or rafts and force anyone swimming underwater to break surface. Fortunately, Black Elk's training had emphasized the art of decoying and diverting an enemy, and

the two youths quickly formed a plan to sneak
around their enemy. First they swam against the
current until they were well upstream from the
sentry. Then they swam to the bank and tugged
the log ashore. The steady roar of the rapids easily
covered the sound of their movements as they
worked their way well back into the dense thickets
behind the sentry's position.

Matthew gathered dry leaves and twigs for kindling while Little Horse used a handful of grass
to dry the breech of his musket, which had taken
in some water despite his caution. When the flintlock mechanism was dry, he made sure there was
no charge in the pan. Then he held the breech
down close to the kindling and cocked and pulled
the trigger.

The flint in the hammer hit the metal strike
plate and threw off a spark. After several attempts,
a spark finally caught and fanned into a bright
orange tongue of flame. The youths heaped dead
sticks and branches over the kindling, then hurried back to the river to wait.

The sentry was downwind of the fire, but before
long a curling wisp of smoke alerted him. When
he ran into the forest to investigate, Matthew and
Little Horse rolled their log back into the river.

They raced alongside the bank past the rapids,
watching the log bang and bounce from boulder
to boulder as it tumbled through. Then they
leaped back into the water and met the log as it
shot out of the churning white rapids.

Once past the third Pawnee, they spotted no
more sentries. But the Sioux village at Elbow
Bend, where they hoped to secure ponies for the
trip to Bighorn Falls, was still far away, and Matthew worried that it might be too late for his plan

to work. The tribe's move from Powder River to the Tongue had brought them nearer to his old home. Still, there was very little time. One piece of bad luck, and his plan would fail.

The need for caution did not end when they finally left the river at Elbow Bend. For Matthew and Little Horse soon spotted fresh Pawnee moccasin prints and knew their enemies were in the area. Again they applied their training and took cover where there didn't seem to be any, by sticking to cutbanks, depressions, and marshes between hills and ridges.

The sun had reached the tops of the trees by the time they sighted the Sioux camp. It was a small village whose people were led by a peace chief named Short Buffalo. The war-weary chief had signed a powerful talking paper called a treaty by white men. According to the treaty, the Great Father in Washington declared that Short Buffalo could not arm his braves against any tribe. But the Sioux leader took pity on his young Cheyenne cousins and gave them two swift ponies.

Sitting astride their new ponies, the youths set out on a straight, fast ride across the plains of the Northern Wyoming Territory to Bighorn Falls. Carefully they avoided the white man's wagon tracks. Only once, at the juncture of Stony Creek and the Shoshone River, did they slow their pace when curiosity got the better of them.

A huge trading post had been built there. Empty whiskey bottles dotted the prairie in every direction. Outside the post, drunk Indians slept everywhere. Others were fighting, gambling, whooping, or shooting guns into the air.

"These red men too have signed the talking paper," said Little Horse with contempt. "Now they no longer live as warriors, but as white men's dogs. They have traded their manhood for strong water."

A ponderous flatboat was moored at a dock outside the trading post. It was three or four feet deep with a plank cabin amidships. The sloping sides formed a pen for several horses and mules. But most of the deck was taken up by wooden crates of whiskey.

Before nightfall, the youths also passed several fortifications the white men called stations, which dotted the plains. To those stations, the outlying settlers would scurry when the red nations were on the warpath. The defensive structures were made up of several hewn-pine buildings surrounded by tall stockades of pointed, loopholed logs. Tall blockhouses rose at opposite corners of each.

Such signs of the white man's growing invasion of Indian country troubled Little Horse, while they made Matthew feel a bit homesick for his old world. Keeping their thoughts to themselves, they rode through the rest of the night, stopping only to rest and water the horses. Finally, near dawn, they hobbled the ponies in a good patch of graze. Then, taking turns at watch, they each slept briefly in a cottonwood copse until the sun was newly risen in the eastern sky, then rode on.

Two hours later, trapped on a stretch of flat plain with no place to hide, they rode into serious danger in the form of a large patrol of white men. Riding with their rifles propped across their saddletrees, the whites wore a ragtag mix of military uniforms and civilian clothing.

Matthew recognized them as the Territorial Militia and felt his stomach knot like a fist. For the

Territorial Militia was an illegal brigade formed by zealous Indian haters, who were dedicated to the total extermination of the red man.

The militiamen raised a whoop and gave chase the moment the two Cheyenne youths veered left toward the sandstone cliffs overlooking the Powder. Matthew and Little Horse knew they would not stand a chance on the open flats. But with sure-footed Indian ponies, they could attempt a daring trick they had practiced while training in the Bighorns.

As bullets whipped past them and raised plumes of dirt around their ponies' pounding hooves, they urged their mounts closer to the sheer sandstone face that sloped almost straight down to the river. The militiamen bore down on them in a thunder of iron-shod hooves, sure of their prize now as the Cheyenne closed in on the drop-off. But their victory was snatched from them when the two ponies flew over the cliff!

Matthew felt himself leaving the ground as his pony leaped. While airborne, he tingled with the headlong, dizzy rush of falling. Then the pony's desperately scrabbling hooves found a purchase on the steep, smooth slope by means of a delicate balancing act. Matthew had to stretch almost straight back over the pony's rump to prevent it from tumbling. But miraculously the pony gained its footing. A quick glance assured Matthew that Little Horse had been as fortunate as he. Without wasting a second, they forded the Powder.

With a ferocious cry, one of the whites savagely spurred his dun stallion until it jumped over the edge above. It nickered in panic, hooves skittering wildly, then tumbled head over rump to the bottom. The dun landed on the rider and killed him even as its own neck snapped like a dry limb.

More flying lead raised plumes of river water, but the two young Cheyenne made it across and raced to safety while the militia patrol frantically searched for a path down to their fallen comrade. Although they had escaped, the delay caused by their encounter troubled Matthew deeply. It was already midday, and Bighorn Falls was still four hours ride to the south. If they did not make it in time, they would have no village to ride back to on the Tongue River.

After the encounter with the militiamen, their only obstacle was a sudden downpour on the plains. But Matthew and Little Horse rode determinedly on through the slanting gray sheets of rain, their ponies' hooves making loud sucking sounds each time they lifted them from the mud.

Matthew's destination was the two-room cabin Corey Robinson shared with his father in a piece of bottomland west of Bighorn Falls. He wasn't sure his old boyhood friend would be willing to help him since he had chosen to become a red man. Despite their long friendship, Matthew feared Corey might consider him the enemy. But Corey was the final hope for Yellow Bear's tribe.

The sun was westering by the time Matthew and Little Horse crested the last ridge overlooking Bighorn Falls. They skirted the town, carefully, and Matthew resisted the strong urge to gaze down toward the familiar building with the bright-green canvas awning advertising Hanchon's Mercantile. He was afraid of what might show in his face to Little Horse.

The narrow wagon rut that led to the Robinson place also passed by an outlying fofaraw, or bawdy

147

house, which the town would not permit within its boundaries. It was a crude plank-and-canvas structure frequented by local miners and ranch hands. The Cheyenne were careful to swing wide and avoid it. But no sooner had they regained the wagon road than they rounded a dogleg turn and almost collided with two men on horseback.

Boone Wilson and his miner friend Enis McGillycuddy had been sharing a bottle of whiskey ever since Wilson drew his month's wages from his boss Hiram Steele earlier that day. Having built up their courage with the liquors they were headed to the women for a little fun. Surprised speechless at suddenly encountering two young Indians in their path, neither man recognized the tall, sun-bronzed Cheyenne as Matthew Hanchon.

"Well, lookit here," Wilson said, his long-jawed face shadowy with beard stubble. "A pair of bucks what done wandered from the herd!"

"And I reckon I know why they're wandering around here," McGillycuddy said. The black-bearded miner was fed up with Indian raids on his camp.

The butt of McGillycuddy's scattergun protruded from his saddle scabbard. Wilson was armed with a Colt Navy revolver. Instead of keeping his weapon in a holster, he wore it protruding butt-first from a sash around his waist.

"These is pretty piddlin' excuses for braves," Wilson said. "Fact is, I reckon these red niggers wouldn't know a war whoop if they heard one."

As McGillycuddy reached for his scattergun, Little Horse raised the musket hidden behind his pony.

Wilson's flat, pale-ice eyes mocked both of the Indians. He carefully noted that the other Cheyenne, who was starting to look familiar, carried no rifle or sidearm.

"Don't miscalculate yourself, red boy," Wilson said to Little Horse. "You only got one ball in that old hogleg."

Baring crooked, yellow, broken-tombstone teeth, in a drunken grin, McGillycuddy leveled his scattergun at Little Horse. "I say let's scalp us a couple bucks. Scalps'll fetch money at Fort Laramie."

Little Horse, who did not understand one word of English, calmly pulled the trigger of his weapon. The musket belched smoke, and there was a sound like a melon bursting open as the huge musket ball smashed McGillycuddy's ribcage and knocked him off his horse. Startled by the explosion, the miner's big roan stallion bolted away.

Wilson was shocked sober, and in that crucial moment, he recognized Matthew and remembered the day at Hiram Steele's ranch when he had practically beaten the boy senseless.

"You!" Wilson said. Then he clawed the Colt out of his sash, cocked the hammer, and fired.

Matthew felt an invisible, red-hot wire crease his cheek. Then the bone-handle knife was in his fist. He raised it over his head and threw it in one smooth, hard movement, just as he had often practiced in the mornings while Black Elk's band still slept.

Boone Wilson's narrow eyes went huge with surprise as the blade sliced into his belly. His arms flying out wide, he slumped out of the saddle and lay dying beside his already dead companion.

For a long moment, the two young friends sat on their ponies. They remained silent as they realized they had just made their first kills. Then, without a word, Little Horse dismounted. He collected McGillycuddy's weapons—the scattergun and a clasp knife he found in the dead man's pocket—as his rightful trophies. Matthew did the same with Wilson's Navy Colt and the Bowie in his sheath.

When Little Horse jerked the knife out of Wilson and made an outline cut on the miner's skull, Matthew felt his stomach surge. But he told himself he was a Cheyenne, and he must accept the Cheyenne way. His face calm and expressionless as a brave's should be, he watched his friend finish his cut. Little Horse stood on the dead man's neck with one foot, then lifted the bloody scalp off in a powerful snap. He handed the knife back to Matthew, who did not hesitate before he too knelt to take his first scalp.

A short ride brought them in sight of the Robinson place. From the cover of a cedar brake, Matthew watched Corey cutting out a stump near one front corner of the cabin. For years he and his pa had been slowly trying to improve the land so the government would grant them clear title. Eventually they hoped to capture wild mustangs and halter break them, selling them to the flatboat crews going up the Powder. But since Corey's pa had got the call and taken to preaching out at the Sweetwater Creek mining camp, the work had gone slowly.

The two Cheyenne hobbled their horses with rawhide and left them behind the cedars. The slab door of the cabin stood open behind Corey. Matthew and Little Horse approached carefully, watching the inside. They could glimpse a handful of split-bottom chairs, a three-legged stool, and corner shelves of crossed sticks, which held a few pottery dishes.

As Corey had raised his ax for another whack at the mule-stubborn stump, a shadow moved into the corner of his vision, and he spun around with his ax still raised. Two fierce, wild-looking Indians stood staring at him. One was tall, the other short, and both were young. They were practically naked, their skin turned dark as berry juice from the sun. One carried a scattergun, the other had a pistol in his sash. Both wore knives—and fresh scalps still dripping blood!

"God-in-whirlwinds!" Corey said, taking a step backward when he recognized the tall Indian. "Matthew?"

The fear eased from the redhead's pale, freckled face. He flashed his gap-tooth grin. "Matthew! Jumpin' Jehosapat! Is it really you?"

Corey thrust out his hand, and instinctively, Matthew was about to reach out and take his friend's hand. But since Little Horse was watching him closely, he ignored Corey's gesture. But when confusion and hurt flashed in Corey's eyes, Matthew finally found his voice. The English words felt stiff and odd in his mouth.

"Corey, it's really me, all right. This is Little Horse. I can't do things like shake your hand anymore. There's things I have to do different now, you understand?"

Corey stayed silent a long time. He studied the bright red line of blood where a bullet had creased his friend's cheek, and again his eyes dropped to the fresh scalp.

"Dogs, if it ain't all good doin's!" he finally said. "Sure, I understand. I heard about what you done.

Old Knobby told me. You really done it, Matthew. A real Indian, by God!"

Corey noticed Little Horse nervously watching the cabin. "Don't fret," he told the Cheyenne. "Pa's out preachin'."

Matthew translated. Then he said to Corey, "Are you still my friend?"

Corey grinned again. "Do green apples give you the droppins'? Course I'm your friend. Why?"

"There isn't time to explain now," Matthew said. "Will you come with us?"

Corey didn't hesitate. "Give me just a minute to catch my horse."

The sun was only a ruddy glow on the western horizon by the time the three of them raced across the ridge overlooking Bighorn Falls. Forgetting his earlier resolve, Matthew glanced down toward the store. Immediately he regretted his action.

In the waning light, he could see his mother sweeping the boardwalk in front of the store. It was a ritual she went through several times a day. Spotting her made all the old feelings come back for a moment—including his feelings for Kristen.

Then his eyes fell to the scalp tied to his breech-clout with a buckskin string. And that was the moment when Matthew knew for sure that he was a Cheyenne, and there was no going back. Kristen, his ma, his pa, Bighorn Falls—all of it was a dream, smoke that had blown behind him.

Honey Eater and the rest of the tribe were the only family he had. If he failed them, his family would die and he would be alone forever.

Chapter 16

Arrow Keeper's spirit was deeply troubled as he paused in the middle of camp to study the preparations for battle. Earlier that morning, Cheyenne lookouts high in the trees had reported the arrival of the final Pawnee bands. And since his sister the sun was well up over the eastern rim and had already burned the mist off the river, it would not be long before the fighting began.

It had been two sleeps since Matthew and Little Horse deserted the surrounded tribe. Perhaps they had been killed trying to escape. Arrow Keeper's heart was heavy with sadness, for he could not accept that he had been wrong about the youth. The hopeful omen Arrow Keeper had experienced at Medicine Lake—the vision of greatness for the youth and the Cheyenne he would lead—surely must have been a cruel and false dream placed over his eyes by an enemy.

Troubled by his thoughts, the old man looked out at the warriors, many of them still boys, manning the rifle pits and breastworks. They had put on their best war clothes and painted themselves. Constant dancing and fasting and singing had left them raw nerved and alert.

Constant fighting among themselves was the red man's downfall, Arrow Keeper thought, staring out toward the hills where the Pawnee were massing to attack. Instead of destroying each other, the Indians should have been battling their common enemies: evil, greedy white men and Indians who did not want peace. War meant great profits for the whites who supplied the Bluecoat armies—and for the Indian leaders who became the white men's dogs and sold their sacred homelands, ignoring the cries of their people.

Once the Plains Indians roamed free like vast herds of buffalo. Those days were gone forever, and as time went on, the formerly great tribes diminished to scattered little bands on the run who had lost their hunting grounds along with their freedom. Yet, was it not the Indian who had first greeted the white men, who had first taught them how to plant and grow corn so they could survive those terrible winters in the new land? Instead of showing true gratitude, the whites had given the Indians their devil water and guns, then watched as the red men began to destroy each other. What sort of bad medicine, Arrow Keeper wondered, could have caused such a tragedy for the children of the Great Spirit?

Matthew, according to his medicine dream, was to have been the last great hope of the Cheyenne nation. When he ran off, all hope was lost forever. Death was massing all around the tribe, and the end of Yellow Bear's Cheyenne people was at hand.

Suddenly, from the top of a nearby cottonwood, the wolf howl of danger sounded. Immediately the village crier leaped onto his pony and raced throughout camp, shouting over and over the terrible words that Yellow Bear's tribe had heard far too often: *Enemies right on us! Soon the attack!*

Arrow Keeper returned to his tipi. His wrinkled, leathery face showed no emotion as duty took over. He removed the coyote-fur pouch from under his sleeping robes. Then he donned his magic panther shirt, which would protect him from bullets. He did not wear it out of fear for himself, but for his people. It was his most important duty to stay alive and protect the sacred Medicine Arrows from falling into enemy hands. The fate of the Medicine Arrows was the fate of the tribe.

But he feared that even his panther shirt would not be strong enough medicine to prevent the tragic outcome ahead, for which he was partly to blame. Had Arrow Keeper not placed too much faith in a dream? Had he not ignored the safety of the tribe by paying too much attention to an untested youth who turned out to be a white-livered coward?

Arrow Keeper lifted the flap of his tipi and stepped outside just as the Pawnee launched their first fire arrows from the nearest trees. The Pawnee did not send as many flaming arrows as they had in their previous attack because there were fewer trees surrounding the camp. When their enemies sent the arrows, Yellow Bear's people were ready. Children had filled skins with water and stood by, ready to douse a fire before it could catch.

The charge had not yet begun. Arrow Keeper

hurried to a rise at the south end of camp from which he could view the entire camp. As he raced up the small hill, he could hear the greatly out-numbered Cheyenne warriors singing the song of battle to fortify their courage.

When Arrow Keeper gazed out from the top of the rise, his heart turned over at the sight before him. Scores of well-armed Pawnee were streaming out of the trees into the sunlit clearing. They formed long, curving lines at the base of the hills behind them, preparing to charge. Even from a distance, Arrow Keeper could see they had dark-ened their faces and naked skulls with vermillion, ocher, ashes, and berry juice. More Pawnee braves guarded the escape routes, waiting to slaughter anyone who fled.

The medicine man's eye was drawn to a lone figure sitting his horse in front of the first line. The dark cape trailing from his shoulders left no doubt that he was the bloodthirsty Pawnee leader War Thunder, whose medicine bundle was the slippery weasel. The hair of many dead Cheyenne adorned that human cape.

Below, in camp, the warriors who were not man-ning the rifle pits or breastworks ran to mount ponies. It did not matter who rode whose pony in battle. Each brave grabbed any horse at hand. By Cheyenne custom, he would not have to pay the rightful owner if the pony was killed in the fight. But afterwards, any enemy goods seized by the borrower must be given to the pony's owner. To his regret, Arrow Keeper did not think any enemy trophies would be collected on that fateful day.

From amid the chaos of battle preparations, Black Elk, his face stern with proud courage, rode to the front of the Cheyenne defenders. But even as the warriors made ready to head into battle, War Thunder raised his streamered lance high. A shrill, unnerving war cry broke out from the Pawnee raiders. Hooves thundered, rifles spoke, and the enemy surged forward as the attack began.

Matthew and his friends made good time heading north to the Tongue. But each secretly feared that they would be too late to be of any help to Yellow Bear and his tribe. The plains west of the Black Hills rose gray and unending as they pushed their mounts hard, stopping only to let them drink at creeks or buffalo wallows.

After a brief council, Matthew and Little Horse agreed to skirt the familiar Indian trail through the rugged mountains between the Powder River and the Little Bighorn. Instead, they decided to save time by taking a shortcut through the unscouted country north of Beaver Creek—country thick with white settlers. They agreed that riding with Corey eased their danger.

Luck was with them until Corey's gelding, unused to the terrain, foundered and went lame only a short ride south of Yellow Bear's camp. Although it had only bruised the tender area between the hoof and the fetlock, the horse needed to rest before it could move faster than a walk. The youths tethered the gelding in graze near water, and Matthew took Corey up with him.

The delay left both Cheyenne silent with frustration and worry. As the land began to dip lower and form the valley of the Tongue, their worry turned to cold dread. And as they neared the camp, several signs troubled them more. For a strange, foreboding silence had settled over the woods and grassy meadows of the valley. The sparrow hawks and wood thrushes were oddly quiet.

As they eased up on the long ridge behind the camp, they spotted the Pawnee sentries responsible for slaying anyone who fled the battle below them, and they made for cover. But before the sentries could notice the new arrivals, Cheyenne warriors began to sing their battle song. Since the Pawnee only had eyes for the scene below, they paid no attention to what went on behind them.

The trio crested the ridge and saw the battle scene laid out below like some grand painting. As they watched, War Thunder raised his lance to signal the charge. The next moment, the Pawnee war cry sent cold dread through Matthew.

"Quickly! Ride like the wind!" Little Horse said.

Having already explained their idea to Corey, Matthew and Little Horse steered their ponies toward the river and the shelter of the trees. The din from below covered their sound and kept the sentries from spotting them. They had to get Corey ready to play his part. And if he wasn't in the right place, all their efforts would be for naught.

The air was filled with the sounds of guns firing, horses nickering, and warriors shouting. The first Pawnee line had formed a wedge with War Thunder at its head. They were bearing steadily down on the defenders.

The two Cheyenne left Corey at the river to prepare, urging him to hurry. Then, as they raced up toward camp to join the battle against the approaching line of Pawnee, they shouted their shrill cry, *"Hiya, hi-i-i-ya!"*

In the camp, the Cheyenne were faring poorly. Black Elk's spotted pony fell dead. The young war chief continued forward on foot, red streamers flying from his lance. Suddenly a withering line of fire from the Pawnee line cut a ragged hole in the defenders. A lead ball shattered Black Elk's left shinbone, and his rifle flew from his hand when he fell. At the same instant, screaming loudly in wild triumph, Pawnee warriors began to leap into the rifle pits and stab the Cheyenne marksmen.

"Hurry, Corey," Matthew thought desperately, glancing toward the river.

Little Horse surged forward and raised his captured scattergun. He discharged both barrels point-blank at two Pawnee who were about to leap on a Cheyenne defender. The enemies were blown back away from the pit, their faces shredded to raw meat. Little Horse dropped the empty scattergun and, seizing the musket from his scabbard, killed a third Pawnee. When his pony took a slug in the belly and fell, the youth unsheathed his knife and waded into the fight on foot, screaming the war cry.

Emboldened by his friend's courage, Matthew drew the Colt pistol from his sash and started to follow Little Horse. Then an image caught in the corner of his eye made his heart leap into his mouth.

The first attackers had slipped through the defenses and were in the camp. They shot children, old squaws, or anyone else who was unlucky enough to be within their aim. Two of them were training their rifles on a young Cheyenne woman who carried a terrified infant. She was running toward shelter behind the council lodge, her braids streaming in the air, but without help, she would die before she made it to safety.

Matthew glimpsed white columbine petals and realized the girl was Honey Eater. He wanted desperately to help her, but he was too far out of range for his pistol to be of any use. His blood cold with dread, he urged his pony in her direction.

As one Pawnee aimed at the maiden's back, Arrow Keeper suddenly darted forth from nowhere and threw his panther skin around the girl. The Pawnee fired from only ten feet away, and Matthew cried out, as if the ball were striking him instead of the girl he loved. He expected Honey Eater to drop, but miraculously she kept on running.

The second Pawnee fired at the maiden from even closer range. But despite the fact that the Pawnee's bullet should have killed her, Honey Eater raced on, still carrying the squalling infant. Only then, after Matthew had spent a cap and cartridge killing one of the Pawnee, did he understand that Arrow Keeper's big magic had just saved Honey Eater.

But surely it was already too late for the tribe. With a wild shout of triumph, the first advancing line overran the breastworks and began swarming through the camp like frenzied ants. Scores more followed from the hills. All seemed lost—until suddenly, like an avalanche gathering strength from above the treeline of a mountain, a different kind of shout rose up from the Pawnee attackers, a shout of fear. It began at the left end of the line, the end closest to the river, then spread like wildfire until almost all the Pawnee were crying out like frightened children.

The guns fell silent, the warriors froze in place. All heads—Cheyenne as well as Pawnee—turned toward the river in amazed disbelief at what they were witnessing. A skinny white boy, his freckled skin as pale as moonstone, was capering madly toward the battlefield, naked as a newborn. His body was streaked with bright redbank clay. A foolish, lopsided grin was plastered on his face. He turned cartwheels and leaped high into the air as he advanced.

To the horror of the Pawnee, the white boy started screaming at the top of his lungs. He quoted Scripture to the dumbfounded Indians. " 'But when ye shall hear of wars and commotions, be not terrified! For these things must first come to pass, yet the end is not at hand!' "

Shrieking, trampling each other in their haste, the Pawnee raced for the hills as fast as they could urge their horses, fleeing the evil spirit approaching from the river. As he watched Corey prance about, Matthew remembered that day at Fort Bates when a half-witted mule skinner terrified the Pawnee scouts. *Stow this lads*, the sergeant had told his recruits. *A Pawnee figgers that a crazy-by-thunder white man is the worst bad medicine on God's green earth!*

One Pawnee, however, was too far ahead of the others to realize, at first, what was happening. Matthew glimpsed the huge black cape made of scalps and recognized War Thunder. With his stone-tipped lance thrust out before him, the mounted renegade chief was closing in rapidly on Yellow Bear.

Earlier, Yellow Bear had been surrounded by a protective band of headmen. But he broke free of them when he saw his daughter in danger. Now he stood in the open, unprotected, staring toward the white boy in astonishment like the rest. He was oblivious to the danger approaching him.

But Matthew wasn't, and he vowed to stop War Thunder from adding Yellow Bear's scalp to his belt. The youth dug his knees into his pony and

they leaped forward. An unfamiliar pistol was useless at that range. Gripping the pony's neck with
one arm, still on the run, he leaned low over a
fallen Cheyenne and seized his double-bladed
throwing ax.

Shamed by his earlier failures during training,
Matthew had spent hours practicing on his own
for just such a moment. Only two in the Cheyenne
tribe, Arrow Keeper and Honey Eater, saw him as
he let the ax fly. A few heartbeats before War Thunder's lance tip would have skewered Chief Yellow
Bear, the ax wedged itself deep into the Pawnee's
skull.

Only as War Thunder collapsed at his feet did
Yellow Bear realize that he had been in danger.
But the chief was too amazed to worry about any
threat to himself. All he could do was stand in
disbelief and watch the Pawnee reverse their
charge.

One Pawnee had frozen in a crouch, immobile
with fear as the evil white river spirit approached
him with arms outflung.

"'Ye cannot drink the cup of the Lord and the
cup of the devils!'" Corey shouted, spittle flying
from his lips. "'Ye cannot be partakers of the
Lord's table, and of the table of devils!'"

Crying out his death song, the Pawnee fell forward onto the blade of his own knife. As he
watched the rest of his people's enemies flee wildly
for the hills, Matthew noticed that old Arrow
Keeper was looking at him.

Matthew met the old man's eyes; and suddenly
Arrow Keeper surprised him by doing something
he had never seen him do—his leathery face eased
into an ear-to-ear smile.

Chapter 17

The unexpected victory tasted sweet to Yellow Bear's long-suffering tribe. The Pawnee had been so thoroughly frightened that they retreated at full speed, not bothering to cover their flight with a running battle. Furthermore, most of them had thrown down weapons in their panic. The Cheyenne defenders were able to pick up rifles and shoot many of their enemies like prairie chickens as they fled.

For the most part, Yellow Bear's people assumed that War Thunder had been killed in the confusion of battle by a stray ax or by a Cheyenne warrior who was later killed. Although War Thunder's scalp had been badly split by an ax blade, it was hung in front of the council lodge on the same lodge pole carved with the secret and magic totems of the tribe. The Pawnee leader's scalp and other spoils were dedicated to the Great Spirit

Judd Cole

during a special ceremony presided over by the
headmen—the same ceremony in which Corey Robinson was hailed as the savior of the *Shaiyena*
people.

The freckle-faced white boy was accorded the
full honors of the tribe. Even Black Elk, Wolf Who
Hunts Smiling, and other braves who hated the
whites came to praise him. Arrow Keeper presented Corey with a specially notched and dyed
blue feather which was traditionally given by the
Cheyenne to friends outside the tribe. If Corey
showed it to any Plains Indian, Arrow Keeper said,
whether a Sioux, Arapaho, or Shoshone, the Indian would treat him as a brave and honored
friend of the red man.

Corey was showered with so many gifts, he
needed a packhorse to carry them back to Bighorn
Falls. A special escort of warriors then rode with
him back to the spot where he'd tethered his horse.
When Corey was astride his horse, the Cheyenne
accompanied him through Indian country until he
was safe again.

Despite the fact that Corey's heroic antics saved
many in the tribe, losses were heavy among the
warriors manning the rifle pits and breastworks,
and once again the men cropped short their hair
to honor their fallen comrades. When the women
had sewn new moccasins for the long journey the
dead were to make to the Land of Ghosts, a small
group of braves silently headed to the secret forest
where they erected scaffolds for the dead.

Shortly after the Cheyenne dead had been at-
tended to, Yellow Bear called a special council.
All junior warriors were instructed to attend
alongside the full warriors and councillors. Matthew and Little Horse, however, were bitter with

disappointment when Arrow Keeper informed them they were not invited. Soon after the council ended, Arrow Keeper searched out Matthew.

"It has been decided by the headmen," the old man announced, "to salute you and Little Horse for your skill and bravery in slipping past the Pawnee. Another council will soon be held to honor both of you."

Arrow Keeper's words stunned Matthew. He was even more surprised when the medicine man added, "The headmen do not realize that we should also be honoring you for your skill in killing War Thunder. But I saw what you did, and I am proud. Many would have foolishly boasted to the rest about this deed. You wisely understood, however, that your enemies would try to use your claim as proof you are a liar."

Despite his pride, Matthew held his face impassive like a seasoned warrior. Had he not defeated his enemies in battle? Did not a scalp dangle from his breechclout? A warrior showed no gratitude for compliments. After all, he knew in his heart he had earned them.

"Never forget," Arrow Keeper said, "you still have many enemies in the tribe. It is true you helped save your people. But how did you accomplish this thing? Through white man's cunning, not the Cheyenne way. Not until all witness your skill in battle will Yellow Bear's people begin to accept you as one of their own."

Matthew nodded once to show he saw the truth in his friend's words.

"So it is," Arrow Keeper said, "that I still cannot speak up for you. If I tried to convince the other warriors that you killed War Thunder, my praise would only further harden your enemies against you. Prepare yourself. The stones did not speak in unison. Many voted against honoring you, and they will surely speak up again at the council."

Matthew nodded again, grateful for the elder's confidence. When he started to leave, Arrow Keeper touched his shoulder.

"One thing more. At Medicine Lake, I did not tell you many things because I was not yet sure in my heart about you. I doubted the truth of a medicine dream until I could find proof that it was not a false vision. Now I have seen you return to fight when all thought you had fled like a rabbit. Now I know the dream placed true visions before my eyes. This thing makes an old man glad.

"Touch the Sky," he said with great dignity, his tired eyes meeting the young Cheyenne's curious glance, "place my words close to your heart, for now I speak only true things. In time you will learn more about yourself and your past. But for now, know that you are the son of a great Cheyenne chief. It is your destiny to find greatness just as your father did. However, even strong trees must bend in the wind. You will face many trials and much suffering before you raise high the lance of leadership."

Although Matthew looked to Arrow Keeper for more information, the old man merely set his face in its usual unreadable mask of wrinkles.

On the day of the council, Matthew and Little Horse dressed in new moccasins and beaded leggings. Proudly, they wore the scalps they had taken from their vanquished white enemies. They arrived at the council lodge together. A place of honor had been reserved for them in the middle of the lodge, one on either side of Chief Yellow Bear. And unlike other councils, when the clay pipe was stuffed with the fragrant Kinnikinnick, it was passed to Matthew and Little Horse too. Despite their stern faces, both boys coughed when the strong smoke expanded in their lungs.

"Brothers!" Yellow Bear said finally. "You know well why we are assembled here this day. Two of our young men have made Yellow Bear proud. They have saved their people and filled the elders with hope for the future. With young men such as these, will the *Shaiyena* people not endure?"

Many of the headmen approved their leader's question with nods and shouts of agreement. Matthew noticed, however, that Wolf Who Hunts Smiling scowled and his furtive eyes darted back and forth between the scalps on Matthew and Little Horse's breechclouts.

"Fathers! Brothers!" Wolf Who Hunts Smiling said, suddenly jumping to his feet. "Listen to my words even though I am younger than most of you. Perhaps it is true that Touch the Sky and Little Horse cleverly tricked the lice-eaters. But women are clever! Have we already forgotten the death of True Son? Remember, I saw Touch the Sky purposely wake a Pawnee. This is what led to True Son's death."

"Wolf Who Hunts Smiling barks loud, but his eyes run from mine because he knows he lies," Matthew said. "It was he who woke the Pawnees."

"I bark loud perhaps, but I do not take scalps off white dogs I find dead in the trail!"

For a long moment, the two enemies shared a murderous stare. Seeing the pure hatred burn in his enemy's eyes, Matthew recalled that night Wolf Who Hunts Smiling had walked between him and the fire. Clearly he still intended to kill Matthew and was only watching for his opportunity.

Judd Cole

"Fathers and brothers!" Black Elk said. "Hear me well."

The young warrior's shattered left shinbone had been wrapped and splinted. Until it could heal, he would walk with the aid of a stout hickory stick.

"During the battle in our camp," Black Elk said, "Little Horse distinguished himself for all to see. His courage swelled my heart with manly pride. But where was How-Do-You-Do? True, once I saw him behind Little Horse at the front. Then I saw him flee back away from the fighting into camp with the women and children."

A rush of warm blood prickled Matthew's face. He glanced toward Arrow Keeper. But true to his word, the old man held his silence. He knew kind words would only strengthen Matthew's enemies.

The council lodge was loud with the voices of the warriors and headmen discussing Black Elk's charge. Then Chief Yellow Bear crossed his arms until there was silence.

"Pick these words up and place them in your sashes," he said. "We have not come together here this day to talk against these young men. The tribe does not always speak with one voice regarding Touch the Sky. But do not forget that at a time when he and Little Horse might have run to safety, they came back into the belly of the beast. This was courage. This was the way of the warrior. This was the *Shaiyena* way!"

Three times Yellow Bear raised his red-streamered lance sharply over his head. Each time those assembled let loose a deafening shout of approval. Only Black Elk, Wolf Who Hunts Smiling, Swift Canoe, and a few others refused to join the salutes.

That night, long after the council had broken

168

up, Matthew headed down to the river for a cooling plunge. As he passed the hide-covered lodge where the women practiced domestic arts, the soft sound of someone calling his name startled him. As he stopped, a hand reached out and tugged him behind the corner of the lodge. There stood Honey Eater, looking like a pretty ghost figure in the silver moonlight.

"Like Arrow Keeper, I saw what you did on the day of the attack," she said, speaking quickly before they could be caught. "I saw you save my father. But Arrow Keeper has warned me to remain silent."

She cast her eyes modestly down before adding, "Arrow Keeper says I would not be believed. He says that my feelings for you are too clear in my eyes."

Matthew was only inches away from her, and he could smell the fresh columbine petals in her hair, feel her warm breath on his bare chest.

"And what is your feeling for me?" he said.

For a long time she was silent. Without either of them noticing, they moved closer and closer together until they touched. Matthew knew that red men did not kiss their women, but he felt Honey Eater tremble when he placed his lips softly against her fragrant hair.

"We have seen each other naked," she said finally. "But I no longer feel shame. I am glad that we have seen each other."

The next moment she was gone, hurrying across the moonlit camp back toward the tipi she shared with Yellow Bear. But suddenly she stopped. When she turned back around toward the shadows where Matthew stood, she crossed her wrists and hugged them over her heart, signing her love, as was the Cheyenne tradition.

Matthew felt his heart swell. But as he stepped out from behind the lodge, a shadowy form escaped through the flap of the doorway, and he realized someone had been listening and watching them. The shadow limped into the moonlight, and he recognized Black Elk. The grizzled hunk of the warrior's sewn-on ear looked like wrinkled leather in the dim light.

"Enjoy your triumph, Woman Face!" Black Elk said with cold contempt. "From the beginning you have plotted like a fox to earn Arrow Keeper's favor and win Honey Eater from me. But have ears for my words. Black Elk gives up nothing that is his without a fight to the death!"

His threat delivered, the young warrior limped off. But his words ignited a quick anger in Matthew, reminding him that, despite the rousing cheers in the council lodge, he was still far from being fully accepted by the tribe. In the eyes of the other Cheyenne, he was still a suspicious stranger, still an untested warrior. Nor could he forget Arrow Keeper's warning that he would face many trials and much suffering.

But as he slipped into the cool river, he felt the lingering touch of Honey Eater's flesh against his. The flow of the current seemed to match the humming in his blood. He felt as alert as a wild animal, fully alive. His every sense was keen to the magic language of the night. Even though he had a long way to go, he had at last begun to feel that he had made the right choice. Among the Cheyenne, he had found not only his roots, but his place as a man.

"My name is Touch the Sky!" he said proudly to his cousin the river. "I am a Cheyenne!"

Don't miss *Cheyenne #2: Death Chant!*
Available in November
at bookstores and newsstands
everywhere.

**SPECIAL BONUS PREVIEW
FOLLOWS!**

Although still not accepted by Chief Yellow Bear's tribe, Touch the Sky continues his warrior training. But while off in the wilderness learning new skills, he and the other Indian youths stumble across a new threat to their people—and if they cannot stop it, innocent Cheyenne blood will turn the grassy plains red!

CHEYENNE #2:
DEATH CHANT

Black Elk spotted something and knelt to examine the grassy bank of the river. Then he gathered the others around him and pointed to the tracks. "Iron hooves," he said. "White men's horses."

Black Elk showed them how to read the bend of the grass to tell how recent the tracks were. These were very fresh—the lush grass was still nearly pressed flat. A short distance along the bank, Touch the Sky and the others gaped in astonishment—the single set of tracks was joined by at least a dozen others!

They reached a huge dogleg bend in the river and worked their way through the thorny thickets in single file. The steady chuckle of the river helped to cover the sound of their passage. Touch the Sky emerged from the bend, following Little Horse, and cautiously poked his head around a hawthorn bush.

It took several long moments to understand what he was seeing. When the enormity of it finally sank in, he felt hot bile rise in his throat. Only a supreme effort kept him from retching.

The scene was a comfortable river camp. There were several pack mules, one of them asleep over its picket. The hindquarters of an elk bull hung high in a tree to protect it from predators. Buffalo robes and beaver pelts were heaped everywhere, pressed into flat packs for transporting. The air was sharp with the pungent smell of castoreum, the orange-brown secretion of the beaver. Touch the Sky knew it gave off a strong, wild odor and was used by trappers as a lure to set their traps.

But what made his gorge rise was the three naked, hideously slaughtered white men in the middle of the camp.

All three had been scalped. They had also been castrated and their genitals stuffed into their mouths. Their eyes had been gouged out and placed on nearby rocks, where they seemed to stare longingly at the bodies they had once belonged to.

The camp was crawling with living white men, who were heavily armed. The strings of their fringed buckskins had been blackened by constant exposure to the blood of dead animals. And while Touch the Sky watched, one of them knelt beside a fourth dead man. Expertly, he made a cut around the top of the dead man's head. Then he rose, one foot on his victim's neck, and violently jerked the bloody scalp loose.

Touch the Sky looked away when the man castrated the corpse and gouged his eyes out with the point of his knife. The buckskin-clad man worked casually, as if he were digging grubs out of old wood.

The man turned toward him and Touch the Sky took a good look. Some instinct warned him this was a face he should know. The man was tall and thickset, he wore his long, greasy hair tied in a knot. When he turned, Touch the Sky saw a deep, livid gash running from the corner of his left eye well past the corner of his mouth.

The huge man with the scar appeared to be in charge. Occasionally he barked an order that Touch the Sky could not hear from that range. Whoever and whatever these men were, this slaughter appeared to be all in a day's work to them. One of the men was calmly boiling a can of coffee and mixing meal with water to form little balls. He tossed them into the ashes to cook. The leader casually scooped a handful out of the ashes and munched on them while his other hand still held the dripping scalp.

He barked out another command, and another of his men began folding beaver traps and lashing them to a pack mule. Only then did Touch the Sky become aware of all the whiskey bottles scattered throughout camp. Spotting more unopened bottles in cases lashed to the mules, the youth realized what had probably happened. The murderers had made their victims stuporous with spirits, then killed them in their sleep.

The scene was so horrible that Touch the Sky nearly cried out when a hand fell on his shoulder. But it was only Little Horse, showing him that Black Elk was signalling the retreat.

"There are too many and they are well armed. We must return to Yellow Bear's camp at once and report this in council!" Black Elk said as soon as they were out of earshot. "I care nothing if the paleface devils slaughter one another. But I fear a great storm of trouble will come—these killings were done so as to seem that red men did them!"

CHEYENNE

**Born Indian, raised white,
he'd die a free man!**

#2: DEATH CHANT
by Judd Cole

When he left the home of his adopted parents and returned
to his people, young Matthew Hanchon found that the
Cheyenne could not fully trust anyone raised in the ways of
the white man. Forced to prove his loyalty, Matthew faced
the greatest challenge he had ever known. And when the
death chant arose, Hanchon knew if he failed he would not
die alone.

WATCH FOR OTHER ACTION-PACKED *CHEYENNE* NOVELS— COMING SOON TO BOOKSTORES AND NEWSSTANDS EVERYWHERE.